NEXT TO EWE

Next to Ewe is a work of fiction. Names, characters, places, and incidents are the product of the author's imagination or are used fictitiously. Any resemblance to actual events, locales, or persons, living or dead, is coincidental.

Willow River Press is an imprint of Between the Lines Publishing. The Willow River Press name and logo are trademarks of Between the Lines Publishing.

Copyright © 2024 by Mark Thomas

Cover design by Morgan Bliadd

Between the Lines Publishing and its imprints supports the right to free expression and the value of copyright. The scanning, uploading, and distribution of this book without permission is a theft of the author's intellectual property. If you would like permission to use material from the book (other than for review purposes), please contact info@btwnthelines.com.

> Between the Lines Publishing
> 1769 Lexington Ave N, Ste 286
> Roseville MN 55113
> btwnthelines.com

First Published: October 2024

ISBN: (Paperback) 978-1-958901-97-7

ISBN: (eBook) 978-1-958901-98-4

Library of Congress Control Number: 2024941059

The publisher is not responsible for websites (or their content) that are not owned by the publisher.

NEXT TO EWE

Mark Thomas

To Margo, Alison and Ralphy
(The world's best wife, daughter and beer salesman)

Chapter one

I'm not working in a Texas Daycare

"How did you know I had a gun?" I leaned across the table, my voice a ragged stage whisper. The world's most beautiful waitress, Ilene, was re-filling the sugar dispensers and pretending not to listen.

Karsci Polat shrugged. "I heard you talking about it a couple of weeks ago. You were sitting right here in this booth, with your buddy, Slick."

He must have been referring to my friend, Sib, who managed a menswear outlet. Sib always wore a suit and visited the barber regularly to have his neck-hair harvested. He was an asshole, like all my friends, but didn't deserve to be mocked for good hygiene practices and matching socks.

Anyway, Karsci had no right to criticize. Afterall, it was the 70's, and he was the epitome of fashion absurdity. He doused himself with Hai Karate cologne every morning, and sausage-skinned a collection of bold paisley shirts. His chest hair always poked through the taught polyester like toilet brush bristles.

Karsci Polat ran the smoke shop in the same little plaza alcove as my paralegal business. He logged four ten-hour shifts a week, Monday to Thursday, selling skin mags, cigars, and lottery tickets. His wife, Tamara, warmed the chair on Fridays and Saturdays. They might have arm-wrestled for the Sunday shift but opening on the Lord's Day was still illegal at that time.

I liked Karsci, he was a decent plaza-friend, but he shouldn't have called my best friend "Slick," and he shouldn't have known about my gun.

I've always imagined I was above loud talking in restaurants, and that a veneer of professionalism stopped me from public bullshitting. But clearly, there were cracks in that persona.

Maybe, subconsciously, I hoped the gun would impress Ilene.

Sib and I met at Miele's restaurant almost every day for the breakfast special, and sometimes for coffee in the afternoon. I wasn't aware that Karsci was sneaking in behind us when his wife was minding the store but, then again, we were often preoccupied, cataloguing every tiny body movement of our favorite waitress.

"Wait a minute . . ." I just remembered something, Karsci was supposed to be partially deaf. He'd told me, many times, about being clubbed in the head with a Russian rifle butt, just before leaving Kurdistan. He shouldn't have been able to eavesdrop. "What about your defective hearing?" I said, narrowing one eye like a sniper. "What about that Russian soldier? Have you been lying to me about that for three years?" I let the accusation drip like gun oil.

Karsci's eyebrows were vultures on a fence rail. "No, of course not, Davin." His voice broke and I felt a tiny spasm of guilt. "The injury is real, but it's only the left ear." He pointed to it, so I wouldn't get the two sides mixed up. "My right ear is fine." His lower lip quivered.

Shit.

I'd hurt his feelings; the escape from Kurdistan was his favorite story and I shouldn't have questioned any of the details.

Incidentally, Karsci sold tons of Hoppe's gun oil in his store and that was weird because Canadians aren't supposed to own weapons. Maybe his customers were using it on their neck-hair clippers or cigar-shaped vibrators.

"Sorry," I mumbled. "But you still shouldn't talk about things like that." I paused for effect then added "especially here." Miele's restaurant was a second home and I wanted it to be a safe haven.

Of course, my gun was unlicensed and the fewer people that knew about it, the better.

In Canada, pistols can only be used for target shooting in clubs, you're not allowed to carry them around like you're working in a Texas daycare. My gun is a Walther PPK, an unregistered souvenir from WWII. Technically, I shouldn't even call it "my" gun, since I took it from someone who wanted to shove the barrel into my ear and help me clear my mind. I should have turned it over to the police, or thrown it into the Springe River but, instead, I hid it in my safety deposit box at The Farmers Trust, along with a hockey card collection and last year's undeclared income.

It was stupid keeping the gun, based on what I knew about its former owner. If someone ever did a ballistics test, I'm pretty sure that the Walther would be guilty of more than shredding paper targets.

But gun ownership was intoxicating. Ilene glanced towards our table and her hips swayed underneath the apron strings.

"I'll try to be more *circumspect*," Karsci said. He had a "Word-a-Day" calendar next to his cash register in the smoke shop and had probably been waiting for the opportunity to wedge one of those lessons into a conversation. "But it would be wise if you brought your gun along." Now, he really tried to whisper, but the hearing impairment betrayed him, and Ilene snorted.

Karsci was the second client in my fledgling career as a private investigator. The short list is mostly due to the fact that I'm not a real private investigator. I run a sleazy paralegal business and spend most of my time delivering fraudulent eviction notices for landlords who are trying to circumvent rent control. But Karsci had watched me solve case number one from his smoke shop stool and thought he could piggyback on that success.

"You said someone kidnapped your dog." We'd spent enough time discussing the gun I wasn't supposed to own.

"Yes," Karsci nodded. "It's my wife's pet, really, a French Bulldog." He pulled out his wallet, then handed me a picture as if it was a clever grandchild. "His name is Blaise."

I raised an eyebrow. "Blaise" was an awfully pretentious name for a *human*, dogs should be called "Buck" or "Larry" or "Slick." He was cute enough, I guess, with his black eye patch, wrinkly snout, and watery eyes. His ears stuck straight up, like a fox, instead of drooping like most dogs. In the picture, Karsci's wife

Next to Ewe

Tamara was hugging Blaise, and the animal's head was wedged between her breasts, pushing them east and west. Tamara was a gorgeous woman, but out of respect to Ilene and Karsci, I repressed the dirty home movies. There was plenty of time for that later.

I'd seen Blaise before; his picture was hanging on the smoke shop wall, behind the cash register. Several times a week, I bought a newspaper from Karsci and the dog supervised gripe-sessions about our corporate plaza landlord.

"And the dog-nappers want two thousand dollars for his return?" My voice was slightly incredulous. At this point in the 70s, minimum wage was $1.55 an hour. Rent for my basement apartment was ninety dollars a month. I probably wouldn't get 2,000 dollars if I sold my Blazer, and it had new tires and almost no scratches. My parents built a garage for a lot less than 2,000 dollars and that included premium shingles and extra insulation. When Sib's cousin got married, his uncle Fahmi didn't spend 2,000 dollars on the reception, and there was a champagne fountain, along with scores of freeloaders, like me, in attendance.

You get the idea; it was an outrageous ransom demand for a dog.

"Are you sure you want to pay?" Might as well broach the subject.

Thomas

Karsci rolled his eyes. "Well . . . Tamara loves him. Blaise is her baby. Most people don't love their kids as much as she loves that dog." He sighed, maybe thinking about his own childhood before he walked out of Kurdistan. "I like Blaise well enough, too, I want the little guy back, but my motivation is different." His eyes flicked back and forth as if he was embarrassed by what he was about to admit. "You see, I've got so much money invested in that dog . . ." He leaned across the table. "It's like pumping quarters into a slot machine; after a while, you feel like it would be wrong to stop, you have to stick it out until the end, and either win the jackpot or go bankrupt." I'd never heard affection compared to a gambling compulsion before. But Karsci always had a different take on life, probably because he grew up trading spent ammo casings rather than hockey cards. Whether Karsci loved the dog or not was immaterial; he didn't appreciate a stranger stealing his casino seat.

I scratched a patch of stubble under my chin. "Why does the dog cost you so much? Do you have to style his fur and buff his nails, and shit like that?"

"Oh, Tamara does all that herself." Karsci waggled fingers that were like a bundle of farmer's sausage. "Blaise has short fur, so that really isn't an issue. Tamara combs him, and I check his nut sack for ticks after walks." He frowned. "Cutting his nails is difficult because Blaise doesn't like anyone touching his feet."

I nodded, pretending to understand, and said "dogs are funny that way." I once saw an Alsatian stick his nose deep into the ass of another Alsatian. I mean, he really jammed it up there. If dogs were going to be fussy about personal space, you'd think that's where they'd draw the line. Here, Karsci explained that Blaise was cool with testicle-juggling yet protective of his *toes*. "They sure are funny," I said again. "Well, if you guys take care of the grooming and front-line health care, what's the expense-issue?"

A real private investigator wouldn't have been distracted by ancillary pet costs. On the other hand, money tends to fertilize human weakness, so it's important to know how it's spread.

Karsci tried to fidget into a more comfortable position. "Well, for a start, he gets special kibble so his farts don't stink."

"Seriously?"

"Yeah, when he was a puppy, we were giving him Supermarket Alpo and the house smelled like a feedlot. It was unbelievable." Karsci squirmed again. "But the real problem is the breed itself, the tiny gene pool. Frenchies have bad hips, so Blaise needed an operation to re-position a tendon, and then treatment for an infection. Frenchies also have this breathing issue, where they wheeze and can't get enough air, so they panic and pass out. Blaise was in the doggy hospital last month and it cost me four hundred dollars for respiratory therapy. He didn't even stay overnight."

Holy crap. Why couldn't breeders produce a dog that was both cute *and* durable?

If a vet told me my pooch could breathe easier after I paid him four hundred dollars for therapy, I'd make a counteroffer *not* to break his nose for five hundred dollars. Karsci was right to use the word *invested* when he talked about his attachment to the pet.

"And you say the dog-napper is coming to your house tonight?"

"Well, sort of." Karsci sighed and shuffled his ass a few more millimeters. He was really giving that booth seat a workout. "We didn't even know Blaise was missing until Tamara found the ransom note. I'd let him out in the backyard to pee, and then I fell asleep on the couch and forgot about him. Tamara was working on the inventory reports in our home office, and she thought Blaise was sleeping in his basket." Karsci sipped his coffee and continued. "The doorbell rang, and when Tamara answered it, she found the note under a rock. She didn't see anyone and didn't look for the delivery-boy until much later. First, she raced around, looking for Blaise in the house. She didn't even wake me up right away, she was hoping the note was some sort of prank. By the time she figured out Blaise was really missing, the street was deserted."

"That was the end of your nap."

"Yeah."

Karsci looked more uncomfortable than ever, as he passed the note over to me. The paper had a greyish cast, a common by-product of photocopiers at that time. I read the demands:

1) If you want to see your little doggie, Blaise, again, follow all instructions carefully.
2) Be at home tomorrow evening, to receive an important package.
3) Insert 20 hundred-dollar bills into sheep
4) Push red button on cannister
5) Release sheep outside
6) Do NOT contact police

"Well, that's clear enough," I said.

Karsci nodded and looked down as if he were inspecting his shoes through the Formica table top. Sib, whose philosophy was defined by menswear, always said you could tell a lot about a person from his shoes, and for some reason that offhand remark stuck deeply in a crevice of my brain.

In fact, as Karsci walked towards my booth that

afternoon, I checked out his shoes pretty closely. They were leather works of art with very thin soles. They were designed for sitting on a smoke shop stool, not for escaping from a hostile country; they didn't even look like they could tolerate walks with a companion who needed respiratory therapy.

I'm not sure what my point is, but it was hypocritical for Karsci to call Sib "Slick" while wearing those particular shoes.

We sat quietly for a minute but, eventually, I had to explain that the situation really wasn't clear at all, that my previous comment was meant to be sarcastic. "Does the dog-napper have a trained sheep?" I asked, "some sort of circus-freak that can transport parcels. . . *internally*?"

Karsci shook his head. "It must be one of those inflatable sheep," he said. "I assume that's what will be in the 'important package' they deliver, tonight."

"Inflatable sheep? What the hell is that?"

"A sex toy." The volume of Karsci's deaf-guy voice actually dipped a little. Maybe he was somewhat embarrassed by the topic, but I doubt it. "Some people prefer …"

I waved my hands to stop him. "I don't want to know how you know that."

"It's a scary world," Karsci said. "A crazy world,

and you don't know the half of it. When I was in Kurdistan..."

"So, you think someone's going to deliver a vinyl sheep-prostitute to your house tonight. You're going to inflate it, then stick two thousand dollars into it..."

"I think you stick the money in first," Karsci corrected me, and a thick finger pointed to the order of events in the ransom note.

I didn't want to get mired in sheep-stuffing protocol, I had to keep this story moving forward. "Okay. Money first, inflation second. Since the note mentions a 'cannister,' the sheep must get filled with gas, like a party balloon." That should have been immediately obvious when Karsci showed me the note, I don't know why my first impulse was to conjure up a live animal. "Then, apparently, you take the sheep outside, release it, and it just floats away." For some reason, we both looked upwards, towards Miele's ceiling.

Karsci nodded. "Yes. That seems to be the idea."

I shook my head. "That's messed up. It's utterly ridiculous." The process was so stupid it made me mad. "There's absolutely no way that would work."

Karsci shrugged. "That's why I'm asking you to help. Something definitely not right." When Karsci was stressed, his almost imperceptible accent thickened. Right now, he sounded like Boris Badenov from the

Thomas

Rocky and Bullwinkle cartoons.

I slumped lower in the booth and scratched at my cheek. "It sounds, to me, like someone hates your guts and wants to make you watch two thousand dollars float away." Karsci's business was doing pretty good, judging by the snapshots of his new house I'd seen; it was custom-built, in a subdivision near the lake. But, like all rich people who grew up getting beaten with rifle butts, Karsci loved his nickels and dimes. Tricking him into wasting money was both clever and diabolical. And two thousand dollars was an interesting figure, essentially a poker bet designed to trap an opponent, high enough to make the gambit worthwhile, but not so high that it scared the victim away from the table.

If I was right, and the dognapping was intended to inflict anguish rather than generate cash, Tamara wouldn't get her little doggie back. Killing Blaise would be a logical extension of the torture, there was really no point in returning the animal.

Maybe, subconsciously, Karsci realized that, too, and was angling for future revenge help.

"Have your neighbors ever complained about the dog?" It was logical that the culprit was someone close. It's hard to really, *really* hate at a distance. "Is he barking too much or peeing on someone's cascading begonias?"

"Blaise never barks."

"Never?"

"Never. It's one of the things I like about him. Anyway, we don't have any neighbors because the subdivision is still under construction, ours is the only finished house."

"Okay." I would have preferred an angry next-door dog-napper, but a similar suspect could be living anywhere along Blaise's daily walk route. Dogs are creatures of habit; maybe he regularly lunged at someone's pet bunny or always relieved himself underneath the same decorative mailbox.

Or, maybe, one of the construction workers in the Polats' subdivision was a psychopath.

I took a deep breath. "Listen," I said, "the floating-sheep delivery method is so crazy you have to face the possibility that the dog-napper doesn't care about the money, he's just figured out a particularly cruel way to kill your pet. There may not be any point in good-faith cooperation with this person." If there was no way to successfully retrieve the ransom, and the crime was solely intended to cause emotional damage, the only thing the kidnappers would return was Blaise's lifeless hide, stitched into a festive Ushanka hat and delivered in a box. I stated the obvious: "You should phone the police."

"I can't do that," Karsci said, chewing the inside of

his cheek. "My wife's immigration status is . . . problematic."

"You think the police will be more interested in her than the missing dog?"

Karsci nodded.

That surprised me because Tamara was so obviously Canadian. She didn't walk around swilling maple syrup like an interloper trying to fit in, she had all the genuine angst and prejudices of people I've grown up with. She could have attended our neighborhood chestnut wars, or road hockey games. If anyone in their little family had potential immigration issues, it was Karsci.

Once again, I wondered if he was lying to me. "So, what exactly do you want me to do?"

"I want you to come over to our house and wait with us for the package to arrive. Then I'd like you to stick your gun in the delivery person's face."

I nodded. That was within my skill set, and actually sounded like a reasonable plan.

The "important package" would probably be carried up Karsci's steps by a commercial messenger who wouldn't have any idea what was inside the box, or who had sent it. Following him when he left would be a waste of time. But if we scared the shit out of him, some of that anxiety might be transmitted back to the customer, who might then hesitate before sewing

Blaise's mug to the front of a big furry hat. I had a strong feeling that the dog-napper was a coward, or he would have already confronted the Polats, instead of attacking them indirectly through their pet. I also suspected that the dog-napper would be lurking nearby, watching his crazy plan unfurl.

Perhaps he was susceptible to indirect threats, himself.

"I'll give you five hundred dollars," Karsci said.

I shook my head. "That's too much money."

Karsci's nose wrinkled as if he was remembering a blow from a rifle butt. "You may not say that after tonight."

Chapter two

always insert the money first

Karsci went back to the smoke shop to tell Tamara he had enlisted my help for this evening. I had to hustle to get to the Farmers Trust before it closed at three-thirty and retrieve the Walther from my safety deposit box.

Then, I drove my Blazer to Karsci's neighborhood and had a look around.

His new split level was at the end of a cul-de-sac that was still in the early stages of construction. It was easy to see now, just how strange the ransom note delivery was. Building lots had been surveyed and several foundations had been poured, but nothing had been framed, there wasn't even material stacked nearby.

Next to Ewe

The real estate world was funny at that time. There was still plenty of cheap, available land, and tons of demand for newly built houses, but the developers seizing those opportunities tended to be unprincipled dipshits who needed to refinance each time a shingle was nailed in place.

I was really disappointed when I saw Karsci's empty street because my only reasonable suspects for the dognapping vaporized. There were no construction workers and no neighbors, either near or distant.

The proposed subdivision was surrounded by abandoned fruit farms and spindly woodlots that wouldn't sprout bungalows until more money was leveraged from gullible investors. There was a thicker band of forest about a mile to the north, and beyond that, Lake Ontario.

I took a look at the Polats' backyard. It was surrounded by a wrought iron fence, waist high, designed to keep a small dog in, not a dog-napper out. It would have been easy to reach over and grab Blaise by the collar.

A young deer grazed in a future neighbor's future yard, but the animal didn't look suspicious. It appraised me with one giant-squid eye then went back to stripping little red berries from the branches of a creeping plant.

Looking around the barren neighborhood, I

wondered how someone had managed to deliver the ransom note without being seen. He must have rung the doorbell then sprinted to a foundation hole. I wandered over to the closest excavation and looked inside. It wasn't an ideal hiding spot, basically, a big open bowl. But it did have a fruit cellar, a little compartment with dirt walls where homeowners were supposed to store preserves. That area was enclosed by rough plywood. I suppose someone could have holed up there while the Polats were running around calling for their little dog.

Of course, the dog-napper would have to be holding Blaise while he was hiding out. Blaise might not bark much, but I'm sure he'd squeeze one out if he heard his owners' frantic voices. That suggested the animal was drugged or already dead.

I checked out the rest of the empty foundations in the cul-de-sac.

No dog-nappers were hiding on Karsci's street, now, and there was some comfort to be gained from that observation.

I sat in the Blazer, in Karsci's new driveway, and wondered if the ridiculous dog-ransom scheme was just an excuse to gain entry for a home invasion. That didn't seem likely. If someone wanted to ransack the house, they just had to wait for Tamara to go to work and Karsci to slink into Miele's diner, then beat the door in with a sledgehammer. Blaise didn't bark and there were no neighbors to complain about the noise, even if he did. If someone wanted to assault Karsci or Tamara, it would be easier to ambush them, individually, in the back parking lot of our plaza.

Was it possible that the dog-nappers actually intended to extort 2,000 dollars from a moderately successful business couple? Did the criminals plan to shoot the floating sheep out of the sky like a migrating Mallard?

The treetops seemed to be gently waving towards Lake Ontario. Maybe the dog-nappers were in a boat, bobbing just offshore, holding shotguns.

That was outrageous.

But once the possibility had crawled into my skull, I had to investigate. I looked at my watch. Karsci could never leave his store as long as one customer was shuffling around trying to choose the right pack of White Owls. I decided I had time, fired up the Blazer and drove to the end of his cul-de-sac. I stopped, just through force of habit, to check for imaginary cross-traffic.

A metal dumpster partially blocked my view.

I sighed and stared at the container for a minute. It was another ridiculous hiding place for dog-nappers, but laziness and paranoia were wrestling inside my head, and I eventually had to leave the truck to check it out, once paranoia won on points. The dumpster was intended for "Wood Scraps Only" but below that message was an additional bit of spray-painted graffiti: "Rob loves Kelly." Underneath that, was a second spray-painted addendum: "Well, maybe Rob should *tell* Kelly." All of the letters were badly faded and I wondered if Rob, Kelly or the dumpster had ever found fulfilment.

Then, the dumpster spoke to me. It was a single syllable, low and mournful: "womb."

Something inside the container had moved and a metal wall flexed in response, producing the sound.

I peeked over the lip. If I'd seen a person crouching inside, I probably would have shot myself in the crotch trying to remove the Walther from my waistband. If I'd seen a mischief of rats pulling Blaise's corpse apart, I might have stuck the barrel in my mouth and pulled the trigger. Luckily, it didn't come to that.

A possum turned its pink-rimmed eyes towards me and bared its teeth.

Even other possums think possums are ugly, but I couldn't leave the thing in a rusting metal cube to starve. I found a splintered board that had once been used as a concrete-form and put it in the dumpster, angled against the far corner like a primitive ladder.

The possum immediately leapt onto the wood and started to climb. The dumpster walls made "ting-ting-

ting" sounds like a dinner bell, so I sprinted back to safety, inside the Blazer. I half-expected the angry creature to leap onto my windshield, like a movie zombie, but it decided to hide instead.

I turned on the radio and heard a DJ introduce a blues song by some old guy named "Junior" Johnson. There was a loud guitar riff then Junior sang about driving his Cadillac down a country road, the wheels spinning on a soft gravel surface. He was frustrated because he wasn't really getting anywhere. I couldn't help smiling because the song was a perfect musical accompaniment for my life.

I was all "drive," no "destination."

If a coroner ever performed an autopsy on me, he wouldn't find any organs, just busy-work wrapped in a sports jacket.

Junior's Cadillac eventually limped past a farmyard full of bulls, rams and roosters, all alpha males who embraced the blues singer as one of their own. Unfortunately, all the males were penned up separately from the females. Even Junior was trapped in his Cadillac. The guitar riff suddenly became soulful, like it was being played inside a dumpster decorated with faded graffiti.

"I'm a ram sheep, baby, I'm a curly-horned devil," Junior moaned, "an' I've gotta get next to ewe." The singer sounded too old to be ramming anything, but blues guys can get away with that shit, they're born with special johnsons that don't rust with age.

I played rhythm on the gas pedal and the Blazer danced past a field full of twisted black pear trees, then past a strip of brush that thought it was a real forest, and finally down a fire-lane that led to the lake shore. I parked, just as a burst of feedback ended the song.

I walked to the very edge of the cliff, and before me was a forty-mile expanse of gunmetal grey water. There was a distant purple smear that might have been the Toronto skyline, or maybe the horizon just needed to be cleaned with a rag. A stiff offshore breeze pressed its hands against my blazer and tried to push me off the cliff. That wind could easily carry a floating sheep from Karsci's driveway to the lake but then what? I looked at the rocky shoreline. There were no hunter-filled punts waiting to take it down.

Miles away, a rust-colored laker was working its way towards the canal, but it couldn't have been involved in the dognapping, even *my* paranoia has limits. I drove back to Karsci's house and found him climbing out of his ugly green Malibu. "Tamara's still closing up," he told me when I approached. "She'll be here soon." He pulled two large paper bags off the passenger seat. "I got us some take-out from the Dragon

King." Then, "did you get your gun?"

I tapped the waistband of my pants.

Karsci unlocked an impressive deadbolt and ushered me inside.

The foyer had a tile floor and there was a powder room in the hallway. To my basement-dwelling sensibilities this entranceway was as luxurious as a Roman bathhouse. There were several formal family portraits hanging on the walls, all including Blaise, but no parents or siblings, just the two smoke shop owners and their pup. Maybe Karsci's family didn't finish the long walk out of Kurdistan. I followed him into the kitchen and he put the food bags down on an island. An *island* for Pete's sake. Okay, Karsci had a tough childhood, but once he grew up and bought a house with a tiled foyer and an *island*, he should have been struck by lightning a millisecond after he called Sib "Slick."

"Do you want a coffee?" There was a gleaming espresso machine on the counter, and I was starting to feel a lot better about taking Karsci's five hundred dollars.

"Sure. I'm going to check your door and window locks. I'd hate to have someone burst through the back while we're all focused on a delivery boy up front."

"Good idea." Karsci seemed to appreciate the faux professionalism. I tried to look half-assed serious as I wandered around. The back patio door was wedged shut by a heavy-duty aluminum bar. The kitchen window had a device that locked it in several open positions for safe ventilation. The living room and dining room windows didn't open at all, and I realized that Karsci had central air conditioning, which was relatively rare at the time.

The downstairs powder room had a fan rather than a window which struck me as an interesting luxury, and something my apartment could have used. Hall doors to the garage and basement both had deadbolts, which was security overkill.

Upstairs, the master bedroom had a doggie bed for Blaise, but otherwise there was little evidence that the Polats shared their home with an animal. Everything was neat and saliva-free. No tufts of black-n-white fur against the baseboards, no headless rubber toys, no stinking blankets. The windows all had decent, conventional sash locks. I peeked in the closet just to make sure Karsci didn't have an inflatable sheep hiding there. I still thought it weird that he was familiar with those things.

Tamara *did* have an unusual piece of lingerie hanging right in front, within easy reach. It was so minimalist and flimsy it was hard to imagine it as a piece of clothing. I decided to withhold this bit of information when I next talked to Sib. I didn't want to burden him with a wholesale update of his fantasy files.

The bathroom was all tile and glass, almost as big as my living room.

The second bedroom was set up for guests, with a lot of unnecessary pillows. The home office was a pleasant surprise, being located in the attic. I pulled down a set of stairs from the hall ceiling and climbed up far enough to have a look. Dormers provided a lot of natural light and enough headroom to play badminton. There was a desk with a boulder-sized computer and a couch for business naps. If I owned the house, I would put my bedroom up here and pee in a bucket. It really was an appealing space, like a child's tree fort.

When I walked back downstairs, Karsci met me in the shiny lobby, holding out a small cup. The liquid inside was very dark, but there was a pattern of white froth on the surface. The design might have been a face that had been hit with a rifle butt, or a blues-man's willy. Regardless, the coffee was crafted with a degree of care that would never be duplicated if Karsci ever visited my place. It was delicious, and I could feel the caffeine crawling into miniature blood vessels in my mouth.

I wandered around the kitchen, taking tiny sips, and nodding at each beautiful decorative accent. The house was like a professionally staged model home. For example, there was a big dish of limes on the counter. No one needs that many limes, unless they are sailing around the world and worried about scurvy. They must have been placed there because the green fruit complemented the veins in the marble countertop.

The house was gorgeous but didn't have much personality. The family-dog pictures and lingerie in the master bedroom closet could have been props in a modern play about an open house. There were a few notes attached to the fridge with pineapple magnets, but even that homey clutter looked like it was cribbed from a Saturday Evening Post cover. One message said "dentist, Thurs 12:30" and it overlapped a receipt for kibble from Parson's, the pet food store that shared our plaza alcove. I noticed that the bag of medicated dog food cost thirty dollars, which was more than I spent on groceries most weeks. There was an envelope corner attached to the fridge, presumably so the Polats could preserve the return address, and an expired coupon from an optometrist.

I'd never seen the Polats wear glasses.

I noticed the name Deanna Lapierre on the envelope fragment, but only because a vice principal named Lapierre got me expelled from Lord Elgin High School nine years ago. I'd painted a rude graffiti message on the gym wall, claiming that the man abused little boys.

Long-story-short, I ended up being right about Mr.

Lapierre, he *was* a pedophile but that didn't get me re-admitted to school or back into my old bedroom in my parents' bungalow, because truth never excuses rudeness.

Mr. Lapierre took advantage of the Big Brothers program to assault kids with mental disabilities after bowling or mini putt games. He'd gotten away with it for years, but retribution caught up with him on New Year's Eve in a detention center washroom. Retribution happened to be wearing a blue jumpsuit, soft corduroy slippers, and carrying a sharpened spoon.

Deanna Lapierre (hopefully no relation) lived in Farewell Creek-Tecumseh Saskatchewan, 36 Frog Lake Road, unit four. It struck me as funny that an address in rural Saskatchewan would have an apartment number. You'd think there would be enough space there to give everyone an unshared residence.

Tires crunched in the driveway. I handed Karsci my tiny cup and he immediately rinsed it and put it in the dishwasher. I went to the living room and looked out a window in time to see Tamara's plum colored Jag pull into the garage. The door had opened automatically. Her vehicle was better described as "used" rather than "classic" but it was still pretty cool.

"Hello Davin." Tamara came into the house through the connecting hall door. She looked at the paper bags on the island and immediately went to a cupboard and pulled out three plates. "Let's eat," she said. "I can't just sit here doing nothing." She ran upstairs to change her blouse.

Then we sat at the kitchen table and quietly shoveled food in our mouths for the next ten minutes.

We ate rice, noodles, vegetables and (probably) breaded pork.

No disrespect to Dragon King, my taste buds just aren't sophisticated enough to distinguish things that hide underneath a crumbly coating.

"Thanks for coming over," Tamara said to me. She didn't look good. Her face was red and she seemed to be experiencing mild breathing problems, sort of like a French Bulldog.

"It's pretty strange," I said, "that someone would target you guys in this way."

"What do you mean?" Tamara put her fork down and pressed a hand against her sternum. It would seem something lightly breaded was trying to crawl back up.

"Well," I said, "it's an overly complex operation. If I was a criminal trying to get two thousand dollars from you, I'd rob the crates of Cuban cigars from your humidor in the store, or steal your Jag, or throw some construction debris through that living room window and liberate your espresso machine." I shrugged.

"Taking a dog requires a lot more effort."

"I don't know about that..." Karsci twirled noodles with his fork. "How would you sell an old Jag?"

"It's easier than you think," I said. In fact, I had a high school friend, Waldy Eckert, who could give the car a new paint job and VIN number, then transport it to a used car lot in Toronto all within three days. "Someone has invested a lot of energy in this dognapping. It's not a crime of opportunity, someone didn't just wander through this neighborhood and notice Blaise romping around the backyard. These people have studied you to a certain extent and learned your habits. They'd still have to do that if they were planning to steal your Jag but, if you think about it, kidnapping Blaise is twice the work because there are two crimes: taking the dog, then extorting the loot. And more than all that, they'd have to know how much you'd be willing to pay to get your dog back, and they'd have to be pretty sure you wouldn't call the police."

It was a long speech, but I was trying to show Tamara that I'd thought things through, I wasn't just using the family's five hundred dollars as bookmarks.

"Well," Tamara said, "We've got a picture of Blaise in the store. Lots of people ask us about him. It's not a secret that we love our purebred Frenchie."

"But that's my point. Someone has to *know* you

pretty well for this to have any chance of working. Maybe it's one of your regular customers, or maybe it's an acquaintance. But it's not a marauding gang of professional dog-nappers, it's someone you would recognize." Karsci and Tamara made wary eye contact as I continued. "The person would need to conduct some sort of cost/benefit analysis and realize that the best chance of getting money from you is through the dog. I've known you guys for several years, and I wouldn't have thought of it. The person would also need a place to keep the dog for a day or so, without anyone else noticing. My landlord would complain about a pet rock." I didn't mention how ridiculous it was to pull ransom money from an inflatable sheep, because it would be embarrassing going into details like that in front of Tamara.

Karsci cleared his throat. "Davin thinks the kidnapper must have extreme personal animus. Whoever did this, wants us to lose the two thousand dollars, he doesn't necessarily want to retrieve the money, himself." Karsci was certainly getting his money's worth out of that word-a-day calendar. Luckily, he didn't mention that the personal animus would probably end in the death of their little dog.

Tamara looked pained. "No. That can't be right." She turned to her husband. "Who would be that wasteful?" I thought it odd that she chose the word "wasteful" rather than "cruel." Karsci just shrugged.

I had a sudden impulse to tell Tamara about *Goldfinger*. In that particular James Bond movie, the evil villain planned to contaminate the US gold reserve in Fort Knox. He wasn't going to steal it, just render it useless. To me, that was very similar to setting money adrift in a floating sheep. But I wasn't sure that referencing an insane fictional character would make Tamara feel better. Besides, if we started talking about movies, we might end up exploring the uncomfortable similarities with *101 Dalmatians*. Blaise had black and white coloring, like those cartoon puppies, and I'd already made internal jokes about his pelt being stitched into a hat.

It was best to focus on logistics. "How will the dognappers retrieve their money from a floating sheep?"

"Shoot it." Tamara was definitive.

I shook my head. "That doesn't seem practical. You can't just blast away within city boundaries. It would attract too much attention."

"Not out here," Tamara said. "We hear gunshots all the time when we're drinking coffee in the morning."

Karsci nodded. "Some guy takes his beagle for a walk and shoots birds."

"Ah!" The Polat's neighborhood contained at least

one other human, now we were making progress. "Maybe, that guy is your dog-napper, a hunter who figured out a creative way to retrieve the ransom money, then reverse-engineered the rest of the plot."

"I don't know." Karsci's face turned into a mass of creases, like a Shar Pei. "The man doesn't look the part. He's a retired typing teacher."

"You know him?"

"Sure. We sometimes bump into each other when it's my turn to walk Blaise. I'll drive him to that line of trees near the lake, so he can crap in a different spot."

"Let me have the guy's name."

"It's not him." Okay, Karsci didn't want the dognapping story to be spread around, that was understandable. But it was stupid to hire me, then tell me not to investigate. Something not right.

"Listen, if he regularly walks around the neighborhood, he might have seen something suspicious. The dog-nappers must have cased the area, maybe even done a ransom-rehearsal with a couple of party balloons."

"I guess." Karsci reluctantly gave up the information. Apparently, Henry Bourne lived on the fire-lane where I had driven earlier in the afternoon. His house must have been hidden in the bush, though, because I didn't notice it.

Next to Ewe

When we finished eating, Tamara gathered up the plates and stuck them in the dishwasher. That made me happy because I didn't know if it was appropriate for a paid private investigator to help with the washing up.

We moved into the living room and fidgeted.

Karsci pretended to go over some inventory lists and Tamara pretended to read a book called *Animal Liberation* by Peter Singer. Maybe she selected it because the title made her more optimistic about her little dog's eventual freedom. If that was the case, she would soon be disappointed. I'd recently heard the author being interviewed and knew that the subject matter was pretty dark. It was about the cruelty of intensive farming and animal lab research.

The doctor who wrote the book described one particularly horrible experiment where baby monkeys were removed from their birth mothers and given robot surrogates. The babies clung to these monsters even when spikes or wire cages popped out of the robot's fur.

Dr. Singer made the world seem arbitrary and hopeless and, frankly, I identified a little too closely with the monkey infants in the robot-mom experiment. My mother didn't sprout spikes or wire cages, but she wasn't a good hugger.

I asked Tamara about the book, just to distract her. I didn't want her to get too far into the first chapter and feel suicidal.

Tamara took a deep breath, and said the book was all about ethics. People weren't really "equal" because we were mixed bags of talent and ability. But we still treated others fairly because it was the right thing to do. Well, she said, the author believed that generous spirit should extend to animals because they were just as smart as mentally disabled children. Actually, Tamara used the word "retarded" but that word tastes funny now, even in the re-telling.

Obviously, she was familiar with the subject matter.

I wondered what Dr. Singer would think about pet ownership. Given his views about scientific experimentation, hunting, farming and fur-fashion, I suspected that he might consider pet ownership a repugnant form of slavery. As far as I could remember, he didn't tiptoe through that minefield during his radio interview. Perhaps, he didn't want to alienate the only group of listeners who might be allies. But if Singer ever crossed that line in his book and suggested that Tamara's relationship with Blaise was immoral, she might wipe her ass with the offensive pages and mail them to his publicist.

Tamara suddenly snapped the book closed and her shoulders made delicate convulsive movements, as if she were struggling to hold back tears. A sticker on the cover of the book said "Brand New Release!" and the cheerful sunburst design seemed cruel in the circumstances.

"When I was young, I used to hunt all the time," Tamara said, "but I could never kill anything, now."

"Where are you from?"

"Oh. Some small town in northern Ontario."

It was obvious that she was lying. I'd spent years listening to deadbeat tenants bullshit about impending tax refunds or insurance settlements, just to postpone eviction for a few days. That doesn't mean I'm particularly astute, it's just that most people are terrible liars; Tamara was pathetic.

Karsci twisted his body towards a mock fireplace; he knew she was lying as well.

"I always kept a gun in the car, just in case," Tamara said. Strangely enough, *that* sounded sincere. "I used to turn off the headlights when I came home late at night, then kill the engine, and sort of roll towards the porch. I'd stick my rifle out the window and shoot at a groundhog that lived underneath our front steps."

That was bold. Hopefully, none of her family members ever sat on the porch late at night to stargaze or have a smoke. "Did you ever get him?"

"No." Tamara shuddered. "Looking back on it now, I can't believe I used to shoot a gun towards my own house."

Thomas

A clever psychiatrist might think the story revealed more about Tamara's true feelings about "home" than her attitude towards hunting or animal welfare. I've mentioned that none of Karsci's relatives were included in the family portraits hanging on the foyer walls and blamed it on Kurdistan, but none of Tamara's relatives were there, either. Wherever she was really from, life here in Ormond represented a fresh start.

There was an awkward lull in the conversation, and I was glad to hear another set of tires crunch the driveway gravel. I bounced out of my chair and peeked through the living room curtains. I saw a crappy brown Ford Cortina with a "Speedy Delivery" sign strapped to the roof. Speedy Delivery had office space at the opposite end of our plaza. They were a marginally legal cab/liquor delivery service.

The driver bounced out of the Cortina, retrieved a package from the passenger seat, then jogged up the walk. I pulled the Walther out of my pants and got into position at the hinge side of the door.

The bell rang; it was an electronic intro to Strauss' "Voices of Spring." What a dick. I mean Karsci, for buying the fancy doorbell, not Strauss for composing the tune. Anyway, Karsci took a big breath to gather his nerve and pulled the door open.

"Delivery. Sign here please." I saw a hand and a

clipboard through the door crack.

Karsci said, "I've got to fetch my glasses," backed up, and the man followed him into the foyer. I stepped from behind the door and shoved the gun barrel into the man's throat.

Cardboard box and clipboard hit the floor as we waltz-stepped back out onto the porch.

"Wha . . .?" I reached around to the man's back pocket with my left hand and pulled out his wallet.

"Where's the dog?" I looked over the man's shoulder, searching for an audience in the nearest little patch of brush, but didn't see anyone. Maybe the kidnapper was a mile away watching us through binoculars.

"What dog?" The delivery guy was shaking.

"The dog you kidnapped, where is it?"

"Holy shit, I didn't kidnap any dog, honest, I'm just here to deliver a package." He pawed at his crotch as if worried he might pee himself.

Karsci picked up the cardboard package. The phrase "Ero-Teek Bo-Teek" was printed across the surface in red cursive. Karsci ripped it open and pulled out a folded piece of vinyl, that looked like a deflated kiddie pool. There was also a piece of paper, a duplicate of the ransom instructions Karsci had shown me earlier.

"Look at this!" Karsci shoved the paper in the man's

face. "It says I have to pay two thousand dollars." Karsci's accent became magnified with the stress; the delivery guy must have thought he was facing a middle east terrorist.

"Geez," the man said, "that's terrible, but I had nothing to do with it. Please. You should phone the cops, right now, I'll tell them everything I can . . ."

"No cops," Karsci growled.

"Okay." Another crotch paw.

"Who ordered the delivery?" I growled.

"I don't know. People wander up to the counter and drop shit off, all day. I never see the customers; I just hang around in the back and play cards until I'm told to drive somewhere."

I slowly replaced the Walther. I didn't recognize the delivery man from the plaza, and he gave no indication that he recognized me. "I'm going to stop by your office and chat with the counter person, maybe they'll remember." I made a big show of looking at the man's driver's license then returned his wallet. I wanted him to think I would hunt him down if he complained about the rough welcome.

"Okay . . ." There was a shuffling pause. Clearly, Jack Sully of 86 Haynes Street (upper) wanted to add something.

"What?"

Next to Ewe

"Please don't bring your gun when you come. The owner has her own piece underneath the counter. You don't want a bloodbath."

I appreciated the head's up. Sully walked backwards to his Cortina and, once he was inside, reverse skidded on the gravel. He roared towards home but didn't even make it to the end of the cul-de-sac before he had to stop. Sully lurch-parked, stumbled out of the car, and urinated all over the metal dumpster that contained Rob's love note to Kelly.

I surveyed the area but didn't see light glinting off lenses. If the dog-napper was watching, he was well-hidden.

"*We* use Speedy Delivery," Karsci said when we were back in the house, "when we get phone-in orders for cigars on Father's Day, or for birthdays. There won't be any record." He turned to face me. "I always have to ask them for receipts, they never offer."

Tamara opened her purse and carefully counted out twenty hundred-dollar bills, then rolled them into a tube, slightly thinner than a Marathon candy bar.

Karsci was trying to work his hand into the sheep but his knuckles were too big. "Maybe you better do it," he said to Tamara, "you've got smaller hands."

Tamara stared uncomfortably at the sheep for a moment. I picked up a little bag that had fallen to the floor while Karsci was unfolding the vinyl and saw that it was a patch kit.

"Hey, wait a second," I said. "I have an idea that won't cause you to do anything … unsavory … to the sheep. Maybe we can attach the money with. . ."

Tamara wasn't listening. She jammed her extended fingers into the sheep like she was delivering a karate death blow to Blaise's kidnappers. The sheep's floppy tail clacked heavily against her wedding rings when she withdrew her hand. The gas cannister was obviously hidden in that appendage.

I'd heard of Carbon Dioxide cartridges automatically inflating life-rafts, but this sheep needed to be lighter than air, not just neutrally buoyant. Then I saw the words "helium cartridge" and "tether" along with "repair kit" on a packing list printed on the underside of the box lid.

Tether?

Maybe this particular sheep wasn't intended to be violated, just tied off to a mailbox and used as a marker so visitors could locate the sex party.

According to Hugh Heffner, modern society was pathologically repressed and needed more neighborhood orgies.

I poked the box with my toe. Our tether seemed to be missing. That dangling rope might have made ransom retrieval easier, but it also might have gotten tangled in nearby treetops.

Karsci took the vinyl slab from his wife, laid it on his knees and flipped the tail up. "Geez," he said.

"What?" I bent down for a look.

"The button for the canister is inside the ..." and he poked the tip of a finger in.

"It's a crazy world," I said, mimicking Karsci's earlier words. The dog-nappers had managed to combine ransom delivery and retrieval with a cartoonish sexual assault. That was disturbing. A prison psychiatrist would need a second notebook and extra pencils.

PHHHHHHHHHHT

Karsci pushed the red button, and our sheep underwent a bizarre transformation. The heavy vinyl mat flopped off Karsci's knees, as if it was a real animal dropping awkwardly from the birth canal. It rolled on the floor as gas entered its extremities. It crouched on bent knees, then rose to rubber hooves, then floated slowly to chest level. I grabbed a leg, spun it around and we were face to face.

The sheep had a comical, startled expression with pursed lips and eyes like banjos. I noticed the mouth was open, but I didn't poke my fingers in because it was staring at me. The animal's back was a quilted mass of bumps that simulated wool in a clever way. The feet were slightly weighted to keep them oriented towards the ground.

Even though the sheep was full of helium, it didn't exactly rocket upwards. The foot-weights were just heavy enough to moderate the ascent.

"I guess we take it outside, now," Tamara said.

I suggested releasing it at the end of the laneway so it wouldn't immediately get snagged in the hydro lines supplying the Polats' house. We walked until we were beside the "wood scraps only" dumpster, then I gave the sheep a gentle upward push. The sky wasn't dark yet, but it was getting there. The sheep slowly ascended thirty or forty feet then turned sideways to look at us, as if it was reconsidering running away from home.

After a few seconds, it turned its nose back towards Lake Ontario and was quickly absorbed by the greyness of the sky.

Later, I looked up the weather conditions and learned that there was a thirteen mile-an-hour southwest breeze, which was absolutely typical for our area. The wind only shifts to the northeast when we get our asses kicked by a storm. I only mention it because it's barely possible that the dog-nappers were counting on those prevailing winds to help deliver the ransom package.

"Do you want me to jump in my truck and follow

it?" I asked.

As soon as the words left my mouth, we heard a gunshot. At least I *thought* it was a gunshot. It sounded a little muffled. Maybe it was a dirty piece of construction plastic snapping in the breeze.

"No," Tamara said. "I don't want you to get hurt. Besides, if we let them get their money, then we'll get Blaise back."

"Okay." I still didn't think a smooth retrieval of the cash was possible. I'm sure Jules Verne could have designed a sheep balloon with a homing device and miniature motor, but ours seemed to be a more basic, weather-driven model. The dog-nappers would need night-vision scopes to track it.

I wanted to maintain a positive vibe, so I suggested a modified form of surveillance. I offered to park on the service road heading back into the city, near the four-way stop, and record every license plate that passed me by.

Tamara nodded.

Karsci gave me another coffee with a foam design that looked like a floating sheep, or it could have been a dead dog. Maybe it was a mechanical monkey.

Tamara shook my hand, and I tried not to think about the lingerie hanging in her closet.

Chapter three

good dog

I waited for more than an hour on that rural road, but didn't see a single car. If the dog-nappers actually managed to shoot the inflatable sheep, they made their escape in the opposite direction; East, towards Hamilton.

But my time wasn't totally wasted, I eventually drove back to the fire lane and, this time, easily found the retired typing teacher's house now that it was dark and his lights were on. The building wasn't even especially hidden, I was just careless on my earlier trip.

When I finally went home, Sib was sitting in his car outside my building. He climbed out to greet me as I parked in my assigned spot, right in front of my living room window. Sib looked stiff, like he had been waiting a long time. He was holding a six pack of Brador, which was his beer of choice because it was over six percent alcohol — a cost-effective purchase when your intentions were clear. "Where the hell were you?" he said.

"I was a detective again tonight."

"Hunting for another porno?" That was a reference to my last (first) case, a search for the only celluloid copy of *Martian Slutfest IV*. Don't worry if you haven't heard of it.

"No, I was looking for a kidnapped dog."

"Really?" Sib was suddenly intrigued and forgot to stay mad at me for having a separate existence. "Who kidnaps dogs?"

"Someone took the Polat's French bulldog, Blaise."

"Oh . . . Tamara's smokin' hot." Sib always bought his stupid little cigars at the Polats' shop, just to interact with her.

"Yeah, but she'll be smokin' sad when she doesn't get her little puppy back." We went down the stairs to my apartment and sat on the couch facing the Blazer's grill. The truck seemed to be peeking through the window at us. Sib opened two bottles and we downed them like we were trying out for the national drinking team.

I wasn't supposed to be in a basement apartment

anymore. My landlord, Art, mock-evicted me a few months ago and we were supposed to go into business together renovating an old six-plex. But Art got arrested for wire fraud and the deal went sour. So, I wasn't movin' on up to a larger place in a better building. On the upside, I didn't have to take group showers or use a stainless-steel toilet like my almost-business-partner, who was doing four years for robbing his previous business partner.

Sib was happy with the non-change. He had an emotional investment in this spot.

"You don't think Tamara will get her puppy back?" His eyes sort of glazed over, like he was visualizing Tamara, rather than the little dog.

I explained the ransom delivery via sheep and how I suspected it was just a way to elongate the Polat's psychological torture. Sib agreed with me that Blaise's future looked bleak. He couldn't see any sensible way to retrieve ransom money from a sheep balloon at night.

Tamara's suggestion that the dog-nappers would shoot it out of the sky seemed even sillier now that I was sitting on a couch with a beer between my knees.

There's a long list of things about my fellow humans that I don't understand, things like loyal Maple Leaf fans, Disco music and elephant leg jeans. But letting ransom money float over the emptiness of a gigantic lake definitely ranks right up there in the top five.

We downed the rest of Sib's six pack. "Why did you come to visit," I asked, "you aren't allowed to stay up late on a school night." Sib was supposedly the manager of his menswear outlet, but his uncle Fahmi still treated him like the tea boy. If Sib showed up at the store after a late night, Fahmi would somehow know and bitch him out, right in front of the customers. It was tough to watch.

"The store's closed for three days. The roof started leaking again and Fahmi's finally having it redone." That was a mixed blessing. Sib needed a vacation from his uncle, but he also needed the sales commissions to keep flowing. He tended to spend every nickel the day he earned it.

"You'll want to stay away from there," I said. Fahmi would be prowling the construction site like a wounded tiger.

"Yeah." Sib shuddered. "I wondered if I could tag along with you tomorrow."

"Sure." We tapped bottles to seal the deal.

Full disclosure. Sometimes, the phrase "Paralegal Services" in my business name is a cruel euphemism. Basically, I'll do any task that a property owner can't stomach and, tomorrow, I was scheduled to rip out a cat-piss-soaked living room carpet and replace the subfloor.

Thomas

Apparently, several legitimate tradesmen had refused to work in the filthy unit.

The desperate landlord was paying me an outrageous 300 dollars for the repair. We agreed to the figure while he was dry retching over the railing of the unit's exterior stairs.

I could throw Sib a hundred bucks, which was way more than he would ever make in his store. I would feel like a big man and have a partner to share the fleas and someone to drag me outside if ammonia fumes took me down.

"Thanks," Sib said. "What do you have planned?"

"The usual paperwork." There was no point in scaring him with the truth.

I had a case of Blackhorse in my fridge, a gift from a client for killing a raccoon with a shovel, so I got us a couple more beers. "Let's meet for breakfast at seven."

We drank and listened to the couple upstairs making up after a fight. They had been screaming for three days and now that their issues were temporarily resolved, they were trying to bang each other through the headboard, drywall, and studs. If they weren't careful, they would gut the apartment. I don't know how they had the energy to keep riding that emotional roller coaster.

Full disclosure time again.

Next to Ewe

I didn't really kill a raccoon with a shovel. I could never kill an animal that wasn't wearing pants, I can't even use worms for bait when I go fishing. The raccoon carcass I showed my client was a piece of roadkill I happened to find. I chased the real raccoon to a much nicer home down the block.

After a couple of hours, the beer had scooped out Sib's brain like it was a soft-boiled egg. The poor guy couldn't remember how feet worked and he collapsed while trying to open my door. I think he actually dented the metal panel with his head. It would have been fun to watch him start his car with a comb or his fingers but I threw him on the couch instead. If he made it home, he would wuss-out of tomorrow's activities.

In the morning, I hit Sib in the face with a balled-up pair of coveralls. I had found them on my last clean up job and they were too small for me, but would fit my new litter-mate, nicely. "You don't want to wear a suit," I said.

"Uh oh." Sib wasn't stupid. He realized that my phrase "the usual paperwork" was disingenuous. Luckily, he'd left a pair of work boots at my place after his last enforced absence from the store, so we didn't have to scoot home for proper footwear. I grabbed a Polaroid Swinger camera from the kitchen counter so I

Thomas

could document the renovation job. The Polaroid spit plastic rectangles out of a slot, and you could watch them turn into photographs.

I re-parked the Blazer in the side yard and aimed the back end at a large storage shed. I opened the shed's double doors and grabbed a piece of plywood. Sib obediently took the other end and started pushing.

Good dog.

We loaded seven sheets of tongue and groove sheathing and eight two-by-fours, plus tools and a few empty garbage cans into the back of the vehicle.

"Paperwork," Sib said, sadly. He knew he was in for a rough day, but he wasn't going to complain. We were almost at Miele's when he asked, "where did you get all the lumber?"

"I obtained it."

"You stole it."

"No, a contractor was operating an illegal business in a residential rental complex and the owner *asked* me to help him move out."

"Are those his tools, too?"

"Some of them."

Sib shook his head, sadly. He cheered up a little when we were in our favorite booth watching our favorite waitress pour coffee refills for other customers. It was strange how Ilene had us mesmerized. We drooled over her every movement even though she treated us like moldy tile grout.

Ilene finally wandered over to our booth. "Hey, Biff," she said to Sib, "did your uncle finally kick you out of the nest?"

Sib looked down at the name stitched in a white oval on the chest of his borrowed coveralls. Of course, the previous owner had a childish nickname. "Fahmi's getting the roof repaired," he said. Sib had once tried to impress Ilene by bragging about how rich his uncle was, but it didn't work. Ilene just asked him for Fahmi's phone number.

"So, you're going to spend the day helping Skippy, here, clean up cat shit."

It was as if she could see into my soul. "Yes," we said together.

"Two specials?" she said while walking away.

We nodded at her ass, swaying within the starched uniform, and watched the contrasting white apron strings swing with each muscle movement.

Bacon, eggs, toast, home-fries, mild abuse. It was the perfect start to the day.

"I've got to check in at the office," I said, after Ilene shamed us into leaving by ignoring our empty coffee cups.

"You know, you can call your phone service from

home."

"I know. I just like to see my name printed on the door." I wasn't joking. Every time I saw the carefully stenciled letters, "Davin Chaney paralegal services," I felt a surge of self-esteem. My parents and guidance counsellors were wrong, I'd actually made it.

The plaza wouldn't officially open for more than an hour, but I had a key for the back alcove, which I shared with Karsci's smoke shop and the pet food store.

I parked the Blazer in its assigned spot by the dumpsters and opened the plaza's rear door. I took two steps towards my office and noticed that I had a client waiting.

"Harf," said my client. It wasn't a bark, more like an old man clearing his throat.

"Blaise," I said, and his stubby tail wagged a little. I unhooked his leash from the door handle.

"I guess you were successful, after all," Sib said as he bent down to scratch the dog's ears. "You got him back." *Scritch—scritch—scritch*. Blaise licked his lips. "He looks thirsty."

I unlocked my office. I had a carafe of water in the coffee machine, ready to brew. I slopped some into the cup I usually gave Sib when he came to visit and placed it on the asbestos floor tiles. Blaise licked it clean. I refilled it a lot quicker than Ilene would have, placed it on the floor and Blaise emptied it again. He only sniffed at his third cup, so that meant he was sated.

"Take him outside and see if he needs to pee," I suggested, and Sib grabbed the leash and they trotted to the back door. I got on the phone and dialed the Polat's number. Tamara answered.

"I've got Blaise," I said.

Tamara dropped the phone. I heard the clunk when it hit the floor, then several more clunks as she struggled to grab it and kept missing. Finally, she got it next to her ear. "What?" She sounded both happy and a little surprised. "Thank God." Tamara must have spent the night steeling herself for a bad outcome. Then her voice became muffled, and my thirteen-year-old imagination believed it was because the receiver was pressed against her chest. I heard her say "It's Davin. He says he's got Blaise."

Karsci got on the phone. "Don't dick around," his voice was trembling. "You've got the dog?"

"Yeah, it was leashed to my office door handle."

"We'll be right there," Karsci said, then he shocked me by yawning theatrically.

"Am I boring you?"

"Sorry," Karsci said. "I had to take a bunch of sleeping pills last night, I'm still a little muzzy. Can you put Blaise on the phone?"

Thomas

Really? Did he think the dog could talk? "Sib just took him out back to spray wash the dumpsters."

"Okay. Don't lose him. We'll be there in fifteen minutes."

The drive would normally take half an hour.

We sat in my office, and I brewed a pot of coffee. Sib drank from Blaise's water mug like a trooper. He was still pretty hung over, so maybe he didn't realize he was sharing. The little dog inspected my hand-forged diploma in business ethics from Texas Christian University, then sniffed suspiciously around the lower drawers of my file cabinets. The dog's upper lip actually curled with disdain.

"You'd better hope Blaise doesn't get a job with Revenue Canada," Sib said.

"Drink your coffee."

The door rattled open.

"Blaise!" Tamara rushed in, scooped the animal up and gave him a smothering hug. The dog's paws tangled in her hair and his snout poked over her shoulder. We made eye contact and he seemed to shrug. Blaise was pretty chill about the reunion, but he might not have understood that he had been kidnapped.

I've heard of dogs suffering terrible separation anxiety every time an owner leaves the room, but other dogs are the complete opposite, they'll nap anywhere and are only mildly curious about who might fill their kibble dish when they wake.

If Blaise was a blues song, he'd be a rolling stone, wherever he hung his leash was his home. When Blaise died, he would probably be reincarnated as a cat. He yawned into Tamara's hair.

"God, what a night." Karsci moved in for a family hug and Blaise rolled his eyes.

I looked at my watch. "Sib and I have to get to a job site. I'm glad things worked out, but we'll have to debrief later."

The Polat family shuffled out into the alcove, still mostly attached to each other.

"I knew you'd be a good omen," Tamara said to me.

"Maybe waving your gun around accomplished something," Sib said as we drove away "It might have motivated the dirtbags to return Blaise, unharmed. Attaching the leash to your office door is a signal, an admission that you've won."

"Maybe." I still didn't get it. I had a reputation as a callous prick in the rental business, but I didn't scare people. Tenants regularly threatened to kill me when I delivered renoviction notices.

"And since they returned Blaise, they must have figured out how to retrieve the ransom money."

Thomas

"I guess." I twisted towards Sib. "But you weren't there. That sheep disappeared in the twilight, I can't imagine someone bringing it down and then actually locating it after it hit the brush."

"Maybe he used a night scope. It can't be that hard, people kill ducks and geese in the early morning, when they're booking it across dark skies." The only ducks Sib had ever hunted were on the menu at The Blue Turtle, but I let that pass. "Shooting an inflatable sheep with a shotgun would be like shooting hobos with a BB gun at the bus depot. The dog-napper might have trained a retriever to fetch the thing."

"Yeah." I rubbed the stubble under my lower lip. "Maybe the two thousand dollars got covered in Springer Spaniel slobber."

"The cost of doing business."

I pulled up in front of the rental house. The unit we were concerned with was the upper half of a duplex so we had to drag the plywood up a steep exterior staircase and stack it in the kitchen. While we worked Sib snuck a few peeks at the living room and his nose started twitching. I thought that lugging up the material would slowly acclimatize him to the filth, but I was wrong. When we started to rip up the carpet, the very first piece of fossilized cat shit that hit Sib in the mouth made him run outside and vomit over the railing.

I watched to see if he lost his entire breakfast, or just the last of his coffee.

Coffee.

After that, Sib toughened up, he never mentioned the fleas that were bouncing all over his pant legs, and when we pried up the ragged hunks of soft particle board, he didn't even flinch. When the house was originally built, it must have had a sturdy plank subfloor, angled across the joists. Who knows what happened to that lumber. I took a picture of the cheesy existing construction to demonstrate that my stolen replacement products would be a significant upgrade. In my business, there's no point in doing a good job unless someone sees you doing a good job.

"The joists are ruined," Sib said. Once we removed the old floor, we were tiptoeing across the bare timbers and some of them were badly splintered. It was a good thing that Sib had wrestled his hangover into submission, or he might have tripped and gone headfirst through the lathe and plaster of the downstairs apartment ceiling.

"I don't think the cat did that." I pointed at one of the damaged areas with my toe. "It's not discolored." I rubbed my chin. "The ex-tenant used to lift weights in his living room, that's what messed up the joists."

"He lifted weights in here? You're shitting me."

Thomas

We tiptoed into a bedroom, and I showed him the Olympic barbell that I'd moved during my inspection visit. Two forty-five-pound plates hung from a thick steel bar to form an impressive battering ram. The downstairs neighbor must have hated this guy's guts. A bench press apparatus was in the bedroom as well. "I almost forgot, we've got to load the fitness equipment into the truck, later. I've found a buyer."

We screwed a bunch of my stolen two-by-fours into the shattered floor joists, and I even used my new level to eliminate a bad dip in one corner.

Another piece of Polaroid evidence.

Sib found an old piece of newspaper in the floor cavity. It must have been there since the last shoddy renovation.

"Listen to this." Sib read an article from the yellowed pages of an "About Town" column. "A sixteen-year-old boy was sentenced to six months in the Sprucedale Teen Detention Center." He looked up at me. "Guess what he did?" It was a serious question.

"What's the date?"

"1961."

I scratched my head. Back then, people were really into law and order, you could get a six-month sentence for wearing mismatched socks. I tried to think of a suitably trivial offence. "He moved his neighbor's lawn ornaments."

"No, he *thumbed his nose at an elderly lady!*" Sib was smiling broadly. "Can you believe it? He got six months for doing this." He touched a thumb to his nose and waggled his fingers.

"The kid's lucky Fahmi wasn't the judge."

"Yeah." Sib turned a little green at the mention of his uncle. "Hey, weren't you almost sent to Sprucedale?"

"Yeah." Mr. Lapierre threatened to send me there before his own past was revealed.

Memories.

I fetched a jug of hospital strength urine and vomit deodorizer from the Blazer. That was another bonus from a previous clean up job. I'd evicted an orderly who used to steal supplies from his diabetic foot clinic. The label on the bottle said to dilute the product forty to one, but I poured it full strength into an old spray bottle and liberally spritzed the exposed wood.

Then I squeezed construction adhesive onto joists and took another polaroid. We laid down the new plywood like puzzle pieces, to stagger the end joints.

"Why are you gluing them?" Sib asked.

"What does the glue smell like?"

Sib tentatively sniffed. "Vinegar."

"Exactly. The adhesive complements the hospital-juice, nicely."

"The sawdust helps, too."

I didn't have to do much cutting, but I always aimed the wood chip plume towards the ceiling cavity. It was like evergreen potpourri.

Overall, the residual cat odors didn't stand a chance.

And that was important to my sleazy clientele. It didn't matter how specific I was about contractual obligations, they always tried to make payment contingent on extraneous things, like the presence or absence of cat-piss-smell in a finished job.

I was really glad I had Sib with me because we finished the whole project in less than four hours, including removal of the barbell and weight bench.

The building owner showed up just as we were vacuuming the clean wooden sheathing.

"Holy shit," he said, bouncing up and down on a strangely solid subfloor. I showed him the Polaroids and explained all of the extra work we had to do to firm up the joists.

"I was going to see about a discount if I paid you cash."

Typical. You always had to be ready with a counteroffer. "I was going to see about a surcharge for the joist repairs."

We negotiated and I got three hundred and twenty-five dollars, plus a case of beer in exchange for a six-hundred-dollar bogus receipt. In the rental property game, you can count on getting forty percent of your repair expenditures back at tax refund time, so the owner was actually getting a pretty good deal.

"Get Brador," Sib said, as the landlord clumped down the exterior stairs.

At the time, it was still free to dump construction debris at the local landfill site, but we snuck it into the dumpsters at the back of Fahmi's plaza, anyway, just to be dicks. Sib's uncle would assume it was the roofers and it would give him an excuse to bitch about their bill.

Then we stopped for a late lunch at Miele's. It was the end of Ilene's shift, but she took our orders for clubhouse sandwiches anyway, because she wanted to end her day with the usual stripper-sized tip. I actually paid her in advance so she wouldn't have to wait around for us to finish.

Like I said, we were hooked.

"You guys stink," Ilene said, pocketing the money. I briefly wondered how waitresses handled tips during shift changes. Maybe Janine, the afternoon replacement, had her own set of pathetic stalkers, understood the dynamic, and was just willing to help out.

I stuck my nose into my shirtfront and inhaled deeply. I could almost taste the construction glue, but it wasn't unpleasant.

Ilene sniffed, "it's something flinty." She wrinkled her nose as if we were discussing subtle overtones at a wine tasting. "Like when you've cleaned out all the solid clumps from a litter box, but it still reeks."

"Like the old litter needs to be swapped out," I suggested.

"That's it," Ilene nodded. "You guys smell exactly like stale cat litter. Hey Janine," she called to the waitress who was taking the afternoon/evening shift. "Come over here and smell these guys."

"I can smell them from here."

Sib sank into the booth; he prided himself on his hygiene.

"I'll see you tomorrow," Ilene said, and we watched her ass move out the door.

"Ugh." Janine threw our sandwiches on the table, but for some reason, her abuse didn't pull our motor cords like Ilene's did.

The human heart is a mysterious thing.

"Listen," I said as we drove towards home, "I feel guilty for taking Karsci's money. I don't care that he got his little dog back, I didn't do anything to earn the fee."

"You're not going to give the money back, though."

"No," I admitted. My principles didn't stretch that

far.

"Then how are you going to make yourself feel better about it."

"I'll keep the case file open and see if I can figure out who nabbed Blaise."

Sib nodded. "Karsci would like that. Then he can go all Kurdistan on their asses." He was back to his old self. I'd given him his cash and we'd luxuriated in Ilene-abuse. "Where do we start?" He gave me a glance. "I can't go back to work for a few days, I don't mind helping out."

"Okay. I thought I'd ask the receptionist at Speedy Delivery if she remembered who gave her that inflatable sheep."

Sib nodded. "We've got to go back to your place first, though, I need to get my clothes. And I've got to take a shower." He didn't like people commenting on his smell.

We got the weight bench stored in the shed behind my apartment, then washed up. Sib borrowed one of my dress shirts because his still reeked of Brador. He also borrowed socks and underwear. He sniffed his pants a long time before deciding they were okay. Sib didn't want to go home yet because he lived in the basement at his parents' house, and he would get nagged for not returning home last night.

Thomas

Sib's parents were the exact opposite of mine. I was generally ignored then kicked out of the house at sixteen; Sib had a childhood full of smothering affection and now lived like a troll underneath the family bridge. We often discussed which arrangement was worse but hadn't definitively settled the issue.

I parked behind the plaza in my usual spot, wedged between Karsci's Malibu and the garbage dumpsters.

The smoke shop was a lot more crowded than usual, and I suspect that word had spread about the dognapping; maybe Karsci's regular customers were stopping by to congratulate him on the happy outcome. He didn't notice us walk by.

The Speedy delivery office wasn't much bigger than my paralegal cubicle. There was a counter, a wall, and an opening to a back section where, according to Jack Sully, drivers played cards between assignments. They had a rear door opening to the back lot, on the other side of the garbage dumpsters, where their vehicles were parked.

The business was about as reputable as my paralegal service.

Speedy avoided paying taxi license fees by claiming to deliver parcels, not people. Of course, if a customer knew the code word, they could pretend to hold a parcel on their lap and be delivered to the parcel's destination. Speedy had a flat rate "delivery fee" that undercut real taxi fares. The company also ferried bottles of Hermit Sherry to elderly alcoholics in rooming houses, kegs of beer to teenage bush parties, painkillers to shut-ins, and medium-sized bags of dope to neighborhood sales hubs.

That was probably why the owner kept a gun under the counter. Some people might actually think that the dope, booze and opioids were warehoused on site.

The company started a few years ago during a province-wide beer strike. The owner had the foresight to purchase a couple thousand cases, store them in a rented garage, then re-sell them—with a "delivery fee" attached—to desperate mill workers. I thought it was brilliant, and I actually distributed dozens of cases for them, back then. I was sort of sad when the beer strike ended, because that connection made me a lot of friends.

No one was at the counter when we approached but Trudy, the owner, had a sixth sense and popped out of the back area.

"Aaaaah," she said, recognizing me. "Sully told me about the dognapping, that's terrible."

"Everything ended well."

Trudy nodded. "I saw Blaise, earlier this morning." She frowned. "Did you really stick two thousand dollars in an inflatable sheep?"

Stories like that spread fast.

"Yeah."

Thomas

Trudy shook her head and said, "that's ridiculous," then had to immediately make an amendment: "Sure, it all worked out, but it's still ridiculous."

"Yeah." I hated it when stupid ideas succeeded, it gave stupid people the wrong idea. "You guys delivered the ransom sheep."

Trudy nodded. "Sully told me." She didn't complain that I'd jammed a gun into an employee's throat and almost made him pee himself. I guess it was professional courtesy.

"Who gave you the package?"

Trudy turned her palms up. "I've gone through the order slips, but I must have misplaced that one."

"It happens." I understood the business model. You can only charge lower prices if most of your income is undeclared.

"But I've been wracking my brains trying to remember who came up to the counter." She shook her head. "It was a bunch of the usuals." Trudy waved her hands at the mall aisle. All the businesses within the plaza used Speedy at one time or another. Even Ivan the barber used the service to "deliver" customers from a seniors' home so he could clip their nose hairs. "I didn't notice anyone who was suspicious." She shrugged apologetically.

"I'm sorry I jumped all over Sully," I said. "I didn't

recognize him, for all I knew he could have stolen the Speedy sign and slapped it on his own vehicle."

"No worries," Trudy said. "He's had worse treatment."

Then Trudy asked me about evicting a tenant who was living in a garage-conversion at one of her rental properties. She wanted to get rid of the guy but was a little worried about turning him into a business enemy. I suggested poking a hole in the insulated pipe that vented his heater. Then, a gas company employee would be the bad guy, declaring the unit unsafe. In those cases, the tenant was supposed to be invited back after repairs were made, but I already had some fraudulent paperwork to cover that contingency.

Another satisfied customer.

Chapter four

Bacon 'n eggs 'n misogyny

"I don't get it," Sib said. "How can you deliver an eviction notice at six a.m.?" We were in the Blazer driving towards Hamilton. I was eager to continue working on the dognapping case, but I had to take care of pressing paralegal duties first. The private-detective work would be like dessert.

Anyway, I told myself that *real* detectives balanced a small amount of glamor with a lot of soul-crushing, bottom-dealing chores. Even Matt Helm—Dean Martin in the movies—didn't always have his arms around beautiful women, he had to occasionally clean bloodstains off his turtlenecks.

We were ahead of the Toronto-bound rush, so it was a relatively relaxing trip. "Well," I explained, "at six in the morning, you can be pretty certain someone will be home."

"But if they answer the door, they'll be ultra-pissed off." When I just shrugged, Sib looked even more worried.

I explained the process, admitting that calling on tenants at unreasonable hours qualified as criminal "harassment." But that was the point, I said, some tenants were unpleasant people who deserved to be harassed. In this particular case, the deadbeat was a stripper, so when Sib rang her doorbell, she would be particularly angry because she had just staggered home and slithered under the sheets.

"Wait a minute, *I'm* ringing her doorbell?"

"Yeah. The landlord hates her and is subtly encouraging her to move."

"Why don't *you* ring her doorbell?"

"Because I'll be re-possessing her car at the same time."

Sib almost choked on his coffee. "You're stealing her car?"

"If a cop stops me, I can make an argument that it's a valid repossession." I took a sip of my own coffee. "The landlord is a lawyer as well as a vindictive asshole."

Thomas

"Why ring her doorbell at all, why not just steal her car and be done with it?"

"Well, as I said, the landlord hates her—I suspect they have a tangled business/personal relationship—and, anyway, there's always a slim chance that she'll be so wasted she'll hand you a wad of bills." I also wanted to make sure that all the occupants of that apartment were fully occupied for the five minutes it would take to boost the vehicle.

Sib wasn't convinced. "What if her pimp or her boyfriend or her drug dealer or the police chief she's blowing answers the door?" He fidgeted in the passenger seat.

"Relax. Typically, those bit players will just tell you to get stuffed then go back to snorting Drano or whatever else they were doing."

"Typically."

"Yeah."

"How much are you paying me?"

"Seventy-five dollars." It was more than he would get in commissions at his store on an ordinary day, but I guess it doesn't sound like a lot if you're worried about being beaten or shot.

Sib sighed, and I could tell he was balancing potential danger against the brevity of the assignment. "I guess, it's better than ripping up that carpet, yesterday."

His throat spasmed at the memory.

"Atta girl."

As we left the parkway, I went over the plan. "You knock on the stripper's door. You'll either get a no-answer, a fistful of cash or a lot of abuse. Then you leave the apartment and get behind the wheel of the Blazer." I saw Sib nodding along. "And then we meet at . . ." I paused to see if he remembered the rendezvous point.

"Rectangle Auto on Hesse Street." Sib rubbed his chin. "Can't I just pretend to knock on the stripper's door? The only really important thing I'm doing is delivering your truck."

"Well, if you're that much of a wuss, there's nothing I can do about it. But where's your sense of adventure? When you're a miserable old fart like uncle Fahmi you're going to want memories like these, something to make you believe you really lived, that you didn't just shuffle through your plaza-life, regretting not doing things you should have done." I was on a pretty good roll and thought about amping up the pep talk by dangling the possibility that the stripper would offer some sort of sexual barter in exchange for an eviction deferral but decided that would be laying it on too thick. Sib was lonely, desperate and delusional, but he wasn't stupid.

"Alright, I'll do it," he said.

"Atta girl."

Thomas

I pulled into the high-rise parking lot. At this time of the morning there were several visitor's spots near the front doors. Sib looked at me. "You realize that this is asinine. The whole scheme is irrational . . ."

"Is it crazier than stuffing ransom money into an inflatable sheep?" If nothing else, that incident provided me with a handy new behavioral benchmark. If *that* worked, then most idiotic plans deserved the old college try.

Sib sighed.

I repeated Karsci's scrap of wisdom: "It's a crazy world." I gave Sib my keys and watched him march into the foyer. The lawyer/landlord had provided a front door master.

I got my tools and located the tenant's Charger in the outdoor parking section. The stripper could have rented a more secure spot in the underground garage, but that would have cost an additional twenty dollars a month. Her car was backed in, but parked on an angle, taking up two spaces, so no one could get close enough to nick her with a carelessly opened door. People who parked like that were self-absorbed sociopaths and deserved to have their Chargers re-possessed.

I inserted the tip of a metal wedge into the tiny gap at the upper right corner of the driver's door. Then I squeezed a nozzle on a can of compressed air. *Sssssssssst.*

Next to Ewe

The air partially inflated a heavy vinyl bulb which, in turn, opened the metal wedge a little wider. I forced the wedge in a little deeper, then squeezed the nozzle again. The door crack widened. My friend Waldy Eckert, who works at his dad's wrecking yard, claims to have invented the air-wedge, but I think he's lying. Years later, I noticed that Auto clubs were using a similar tool to open car doors for careless owners, but Waldy didn't seem to be collecting royalties. Waldy wore rubber boots to his cousin's wedding.

The door crack was now wide enough for me to manipulate an oil dipstick with a bent tip. *That* burglary tool was my invention. An oil dipstick is the flattest, strongest, most flexible piece of metal you'll ever find in close proximity to the car you're trying to steal. In those days, hoods didn't lock, they could be opened from the outside, so every car came equipped with its own theft device. The air-wedge made it a lot easier to manipulate, however.

I got the dipstick hooked onto the button flange, pulled up, and I was inside.

You've probably seen movies where thieves rip a plastic cowling off the steering column and cross a couple of wires to start a vehicle.

Well, I can't do that. Waldy tried to teach me, but I never had the patience, the inclination, or the fine motor skill. Instead, I hammered a cheap screwdriver into the ignition. It's simple and effective and car manufacturers wouldn't be able to outsmart it until they invented transponders, decades later.

I twisted the pseudo key and the Charger started right up, with an unnecessary blast of muffler noise. It was one more reason to dislike the car owner and justify the liberation.

I tapped the gas pedal like a cat, but tires still spun and the car lurched forward. It was a lot different than driving the Blazer. Sometimes when I stomped on my truck's gas pedal, nothing at all happened and I would have to write the vehicle a friendly note asking it to speed up.

I was just getting the hang of the power surges when I reached Rectangle. An employee unlocked a rolling gate to let me in the compound. He flicked a cigarette onto the ground indicating the spot where I was to park. Then, he gave me a two-fingered salute but never asked for any paperwork. "I left the keys inside," I said as I walked through the gate, and he just smiled. I played with the change in my pockets for a minute or so, then Sib pulled up in the Blazer. He looked haggard, so I knew he had actually knocked on the tenant's door and experienced some sort of interaction.

I slid into the driver's seat, and he moved out of the

way, along the bench. "So," I said, "what happened."

Sib just looked at me for a long time. Eventually, as I turned onto the highway he asked, "how do you sleep at night?" It's funny. We talk about a lot of extremely personal things—we caught VD from the same girl—but he never told me what happened when that apartment door opened. I always thought it would slip out after a few high-test Bradors, but it never did.

I turned the radio up when Junior Johnson's "Gotta get next to Ewe" came on. I sang along, while Sib cringed in the corner.

I don't know if he just didn't like the song, or if maybe the stripper assaulted him with an inflatable ram.

By the time we got back to Ormond it was time for breakfast. We slid into our regular booth at Miele's and Ilene ignored us for as long as she could. I didn't mind the delay because we had a lot of time to kill before the library opened. I'd decided to do a little research and see if dognapping was actually a thing. To be honest, I'd only heard of it in connection with Cruella De-Ville's puppy collection, and I had trouble believing any non-cartoon criminal would do it.

When Ilene finally approached with the coffee pot, I asked her if she had ever heard of a dog being kidnapped.

She surprised me by nodding. "Yeah. Someone took

Thomas

my uncle's Scotty. Left a ransom note and everything."

"Really? What happened?"

"Someone saw the guy taking Hamish for a walk and told my uncle about it. My uncle waited until the guy went to work, then kicked the door in and took the puppy back."

"Did he phone the police?"

"Nah."

"Why not?" Sib was looking for a chance to inject himself into the conversation.

Ilene placed one hand on her hip and dangled the carafe from the other. "There must have been some history between them."

"So, it wasn't an actual dognapping for profit, the person was doing it because he hated your uncle."

"I guess." Ilene didn't see the distinction, but it was important to me. I believed that the criminals who took Blaise weren't primarily interested in the ransom but, of course, I couldn't prove that, since the money had been harvested and the little dog returned.

"The usual," Ilene said. It was more of a statement than a question.

I bought Sib another bacon, egg, 'n misogyny special. Sib would typically pay during Christmas, the lead up to father's-day, prom month, and the fall job hunt season. His commissions peaked at weird times.

When Ilene delivered our food, she told Sib "Your uncle was freaking out at the roofers yesterday."

"What happened?"

"I think he fired them. I saw them packing up."

Uh oh. Maybe dumping my construction garbage in Fahmi's bin was a bad decision.

"One of them went through the roof," Ilene said, over her shoulder.

Oh, good. The dispute wasn't about anything I had done, but about a catastrophic personal injury. It's amazing how little snippets of information can either darken or brighten your day.

We ate and toyed with a rare coffee re-fill.

Finally, it was nine thirty and the library was open. I parked the Blazer outside because the underground lot usually smelled like yesterday's rental unit. I'm not sure Sib had ever been inside the library before, because I had to point out that the reference section was upstairs. He was fixated on the homeless alcove where *anyone* could sit and read the free newspapers. It was also the only place in the library where you were allowed to drink coffee and leave crumbs on the floor.

I've spent a lot of time in the library's reference section tracking down deadbeat tenants with various city directories. The Librarian, Maggie Haberman, always treated my enquiries like they were serious academic research and never made snide comments about the sleaziness of my profession. I wondered if they taught that brand of politeness in Librarian school.

Maggie also liked me because I returned all of the library books I found abandoned in rental units. Usually those books were stolen, rather than simply unreturned. This happened before books could be electronically scanned and libraries operated mostly on the honor system.

Today, I announced that I wanted to research dognapping and Maggie told us to have a seat at one of the tables. Within a couple of minutes, she returned with three encyclopedias opened to the proper sections and a spiral-bound report that looked like a school project.

I took the encyclopedias; Sib took the report (which was a PhD thesis).

We quickly learned that dognapping had an impressive pedigree.

In the late eighteen-hundreds, dogs were stolen and sold for sled teams during various gold rushes. I suddenly remembered reading *Call of the Wild* in grade eight English class. The main character was a Saint Bernard named "Buck," stolen from his yard in California and shipped to Alaska. Apparently, dognapping was a common prank in the 1930s, although it's hard to imagine why anyone would think that sort of thing was funny. The practice became monetized several decades later. In 1965, dog-nappers were targeting Greyhounds because those animals were capable of generating a lot of prize money. Clever criminals recognized the benefit of a regular paycheck over a one-off theft. The Britannica article had an account of a particularly fast dog named Hi Joe, valued at $14,000 who was taken from his London kennel and smuggled to Scotland.

In June of that same year, a stolen Dalmatian died during experimental heart surgery in a New York hospital. That stunned me because I thought modern medicine was decades removed from that type of body-harvesting.

I wondered if some crazed scientist would ever kidnap a wheezy French Bulldog to test sketchy respiratory medicines.

Apparently, unethical medical research was such a big problem, it spawned new legislation, The Animal Welfare Act, which was supposed to blunt the Frankenstein-animal-trade. But dog-nappers still operated, they merely re-focused their energies on supplying unscrupulous pet stores. These days, owners can tattoo their pet's ears, or have them microchipped. But back then, it was tough to definitively identify a pet once its tag and collar had been removed.

Thomas

The world Book told the story of a famous NASCAR driver who paid a $1,000 reward for his "missing" dog. The animal was returned by three men who claimed to have seen the animal wandering around just a few minutes after they saw its reward poster. Police assumed those men stole the pet, then waited for the reward to be advertised. The pet owner said, in retrospect, it was suspicious that good Samaritans covered their car's licence plate with a paper bag.

I thought the "reward" scam was brilliant because it removed the danger associated with outright criminality, in particular, the vulnerability of collecting cash at a ransom drop.

That strategy might have worked in Blaise's case, although I doubt the Polats would have immediately offered two thousand for his return.

The thesis Sib was reading was a detailed study of dognapping in Chicago. By 1974, more than a hundred dogs per month were being taken and held for ransom in that one city. It was a regionalized niche crime. The PhD candidate speculated that Chicago criminals had a long history of dog-stealing, starting when they were children, using emotional blackmail to extort candy-money from pet owners. Some childhood gangs even employed cherubic toddlers who were able to cry on command and pretended to be heartbroken when the stolen dogs were returned.

Eventually, I'd had enough, and Maggie re-shelved my encyclopedias. I had to admit it was wrong to automatically discount dognapping as a professional criminals' activity. Maybe it really was straightforward mathematics: Blaise equals two thousand dollars. If that was the case, the only mystery was why insist on an inflatable sheep for ransom transport.

As always, I asked Maggie if she had any new library equipment and she pointed to a printer, which was half the size of a daisywheel monstrosity in my office. Maggie offered to demonstrate its remarkable abilities by printing me a business card, which I found utterly amazing. My printer could only handle full sized sheets with a strip of punched feeder holes in the margins, and sloppy, serrated tear-offs. Maggie filled out a template, while I dictated. I had her put both "private investigator" and "paralegal services" underneath my name, as well as include my phony degree in business ethics from Texas Christian University. The printer whirred in an adjacent cubby-hole.

Maggie fetched the card, which had the textured look of traditionally engraved products.

Sib was impressed and got Maggie to print him a card for his clothing store that said "Manager" rather than "Sales Associate."

Thomas

It was a nice thing to do, and Maggie always had an aggressive customers-first philosophy, but I knew something was up. She wanted to broach a subject outside ordinary library business, and was trying to work up the nerve.

Finally, "it's odd," Maggie said, "that you guys are interested in dognapping. We found a dognapping ransom note in the copier tray just the other day." Sib and I glanced at each other while Maggie rooted around in the top drawer of her desk. She pulled out a sheaf of papers and handed one to me:

1) If you want to see your little doggie, Blaise, again, follow all instructions carefully.
2) Be at home tomorrow evening, to receive an important package.
3) Insert 20 hundred-dollar bills into sheep
4) Push red button on cannister
5) Release sheep outside
6) Do NOT contact police

"That's Karsci's note," I told Sib.

"So, it's real?" Maggie asked, eagerly, "there was a real dognapping?"

"Yeah. A friend of ours had his French Bulldog taken. It was just returned yesterday."

Maggie snorted. "I phoned the police when Shelly

found this on the Xerox glass, but they said it was a joke. They said it was impractical to deliver money in a sheep's . . ." her voice faded; she was unwilling to name the particular anatomical pouch.

"Yeah, I thought there was something fishy about it, too."

"Are all those papers the same?" Sib pointed at the bundle in her hand.

"Yes. They were in that trash can, next to the copier." She showed us the stack of identical messages.

"Why did the person make so many?"

"Well . . ." Maggie's voice became conspiratorial "I think he was trying to make the image fuzzier by copying a copy of a copy of a copy. Do you see what I mean?"

I scratched my ear. "To disguise the typing?"

"Yes." Maggie was delighted that the phrase "private investigator" on my new business card was appropriate. "I'm sure the person typed the message on one of our machines." She pointed to a bank of Underwoods on the other side of the room.

"It was careless of the person to leave those copies lying around."

"That's exactly what the policeman said!" Maggie sounded triumphant. "That's what made him think it was a prank! I told him that leaving the copies behind may have been a deliberate part of the plan, like a double bluff, but the officer got snippy with me, so I hung up."

"Do you mind if I keep these?"

"Not at all." Maggie placed them inside a file folder and gave it to me.

"Did you see who made the copies?"

"No, I didn't."

"But you said 'he.'"

Maggie's lips became as thin as the coils of a paperclip. She didn't like her pronoun choice to be questioned. "It was a matter of convenience. I didn't actually see the person."

"Someone paying for thirty or forty copies didn't stand out?"

"Oh no. Sometimes students copy *entire textbooks*. We're not supposed to let them, but how can we possibly police it?"

"But *why* would the kidnappers leave those papers behind?" Sib asked. "What would it accomplish?"

Maggie glanced at another librarian who was sitting at the central information desk. Eventually, we stared at the woman as well. "Shelly was the one who found the note, and she was *very* interested in it." There was a pause, then Maggie repeated "*Very* interested."

Ordinarily, Maggie didn't let gossipy accusations hang in the air like overdue fines. I had to decode the silence. "Do you think Shelly wrote the note, herself, then just pretended to find it? Or do you mean, there was some benefit to *letting* Shelly find it?"

"I'm sure I can't say," Maggie sniffed. She obviously didn't like her co-worker.

I looked at the back of Shelly's head; it didn't look like a dog-napper's scalp. "Maybe I'll ask her."

"Maybe you should," Maggie said.

"Thanks." We circled the information desk like big game hunters. "Mrs. Ionides," I said. Maggie hadn't mentioned Shelly's surname, but there was a little nameplate on her desk.

"Yezzah." Some people can make the simplest words sound complicated.

"I understand you found a dognapping note on the copier glass two days ago."

"Yezzenno." (That's the last time I'll try to reproduce her weird noises.) She looked up. "The papers were lying on my desk when I came back from a break. A patron found them and left me a little note."

Cool. More evidence. "Could I see that note?"

"No. I didn't think it was important until Maggie wanted to call the police. I didn't keep the note."

"You didn't think it was a serious ransom demand?"

"No." Then she smiled like a cat who sees a wounded bird. "But I thought it would be a wonderful promotion for the hunting and fishing club."

"Kidnapping a pet?"

"No." laugh/snort. "I meant stuffing some sort of prize into an animal balloon then releasing it. People could track the balloon and shoot it down to retrieve the prize." Her gaze tilted upwards. "It would work especially well with our junior gunslingers."

"Wouldn't that be a little dangerous?" I thought the idea was absolutely insane.

"It would have to be done on a large tract of private land. But a number of local farmers cooperate with us during the fall hunt." She tapped her teeth with a pencil eraser. "Yes, I think it would work very well."

I didn't know what to say. I looked at Sib but he was playing with the rolled-up PhD proposal and trying not to look horrified.

"I'm the Hunting and Fishing Club's publicity secretary." Mrs. Ionides announced. "Last year, we tagged a trout in our pond for junior anglers' day, but no one could redeem the prize because no one caught it. Later we found the tag in a pile of animal scat. A marmot or a mink beat the fisherman to it. I don't know why that stupid animal couldn't have eaten another fish; he ruined the promotion." She leaned toward us aggressively and the pencil quivered with anticipation. "But this balloon animal idea. . . this has real potential."

I wanted to ask what Marmot shit looked like but Sib ducked in front of me with a more sensible question. "Has anyone else at your club ever mentioned balloon animals?" He and I must have been limping towards the same conclusion, a possibility that would have been obvious to real detectives a long time ago: the dognapper might well be a local, experienced hunter, perfectly comfortable with the prospect of blasting a money-stuffed pinata out of the troposphere. Until Mrs. Ionides' eagerly embraced the idea, we couldn't take it seriously.

Now we had a hunting-and-fishing-club full of viable suspects.

"No one's mentioned an animal balloon!" the librarian snorted. She didn't like being accused of plagiarism. "I thought of the promotion, my*self*." Sib nudged me. He thought she was lying.

"Where's the Hunting and Fishing Club?" I asked.

"Are you interested in joining?"

That's the difference between people. When I asked Maggie Haberman for information about dognapping, she didn't immediately ask me if I was interested in stealing a pet.

"Sure," I said. "I have a pistol and should probably learn how to shoot the thing."

Mrs. Ionides produced a pamphlet like a street

magician pulling a bird from a child's hair.

I took the piece of paper. "Thank you."

Sib put his PhD-in-dognapping-proposal on the desk with a flourish and we left the building like Elvis.

"Do you want to lift fingerprints from those photocopy papers?" Sib's question wasn't as silly as it sounded. We once did a project where we took our science teacher's prints off a beer bottle (you were allowed to use classroom props like that at one time) and transferred the pattern to an overhead slide. We knew how to do it.

"Nah." I shook my head. "It isn't practical. After eliminating you, me, and the two librarians, we'd just end up accusing some guy who works the night shift at a paper warehouse." Now that I was a private investigator with a business card, I needed to focus on my core skills. I wasn't a detail-oriented forensics man, I was more of a big-picture guy.

We had to take another break from sleuthing so I could accomplish a bill-paying paralegal task. A client had asked me to deliver another sketchy eviction notice and I figured it would be good theatre to have a well-dressed foreign-looking guy standing beside me. Supposedly, the building owner was going to move into the little rental unit, himself, and treat it as his primary residence.

Next to Ewe

That story was marmot shit, and everybody knew it; the owner just wanted to sell an empty house. It's always easier to sell a bridge without a troll but, more to the point, rent control legislation allows a generous re-set when a fresh owner takes over an unoccupied building.

The eviction was actually plan-B, the owner originally wanted me to drag the tenant out his bathroom window and chuck all his possessions into a nearby ditch.

But I demurred.

That strategy only works with people who have closets full of skeletons, people who can't afford to tell a policeman their side of the dispute. Normal people can't be assaulted or threatened in such a cavalier way.

Sometimes, you need to build a box, then think outside it.

In this particular instance, I wanted to offer the tenant a new home with another one of my clients, who was experiencing problems with his in-law suite. That unit's "legal-nonconforming" status had lapsed while it sat empty for some repairs.

But if I could find someone who would swear they had continuously lived in the unit throughout the renovations, the problem would be rectified. In return for lying under oath, the prospective tenant would get a substantial bonus, say three months' free rent.

Thomas

I presented that scenario to the tenant I was evicting and juxtaposed it with the prolonged legal root-canal he could expect from a dispute with his current landlord. The tenant hesitated, but when Sib leaned in and asked him if he'd like to inspect his new home prior to moving in, I knew the guy was hooked. Sib could always close a deal; it didn't matter if he was selling a silk purse or a sow's ear.

The only thing Sib couldn't sell was himself.

It took about three hours to button everything up. I even offered to help if the tenant wanted to lodge an official complaint against his old landlord. When we were done, Sib had a little more respect for me as a businessman.

At least we weren't shredding stained carpets and stealing cars.

I wondered what Hercule Poirot did to occupy his downtime between deductions.

We were heading back to Miele's for a celebratory coffee and Danish when we happened to pass by the Ero-Teek Bo-Teek. It was a moderately grubby storefront on Prince Albert Street, between a plumbing supply warehouse and a Serpentarium. (For those of you who don't know, that would be a store that sells snakes.) Not sure why, but I'd never been in this neighborhood before. It was more than sleazy enough to generate my brand of paralegal work, but so far, I hadn't had the pleasure.

I'd investigated Speedy Delivery's connection to the inflatable sheep but hadn't thought about going right to the retail source. It's strange, but hunting for the store just never occurred to me. Maybe I wasn't a big-picture detective after all.

But now that I'd tripped over the clue, we might as well stop and ask the proprietor about recent inflatable-sheep customers.

The Ero-Teek Bo-Teek had a large front window with female mannequins dressed in tacky lingerie. I'm pretty sure that one of the mannequins was wearing the furry red number that was hanging in Tamara Polat's closet.

I tried to redeem myself by making a few clever Sherlock Holmes assumptions:

1) Most of the Ero-Teek Bo-teek's customers were men.
2) Karsci did all of his Valentine's Day shopping there.
3) Before Blaise got dog-napped and ruined everything, Karsci had been hoping Tamara would slither into the red, furry lingerie, and that's why it had been positioned front

and center in the closet.

I also wondered if *Karsci* was the person who purchased the inflatable sheep.

That suspicion was unreasonable, because Karsci had appealed for my help with the dognapping, and his distress seemed genuine. But my paralegal business has conditioned me to think the worst of people. Maybe Karsci wasn't enamored with Blaise and his respiratory therapy bills and would have quietly welcomed a reduction in their happy little family. Dragging me into the affair was just a twisted declaration of his innocence.

Like I said, it was ridiculous, because if Blaise disappeared, Tamara would be distraught and furry-lingerie-wearing might cease altogether.

I parked in front of the serpentarium and noticed an odd sign in the window: "Feeding time: 4:30." Why would they advertise household chores like that?

We sheepishly walked into the Bo-Teek.

A tall, skinny woman looked up from a cash register and said "hello."

"Hello," we mumbled back.

"If you need any help, just give me a shout." Her head dipped as she wrestled a strip of paper through a cash register slot.

Sib and I pretended to shop. There were two central

aisles full of fishnet clothing, a rack full of magazines that put Karsci's skin rags to shame, a side wall full of "toys," and the front window mannequins that could stop traffic.

For some reason, I wasn't able to enjoy the experience. Maybe I was embarrassed to see the contents of my own psychological junk drawers spilled out in the open.

"Hey, check this out," Sib said, holding up a brightly colored cardboard box he'd found in the "toys" section.

I read the label. "Dial-a-Feel Ultimate Pleasure Device." There was an illustration of the product, focusing on an over-sized control panel. Basically, the thing was a cube with a hole in it.

"Geez," Sib said, "Listen to this." He cleared his throat and read a blurb from the side of the package: "You're a busy, important man, you don't have time to waste on the superficial politeness of mixers, or the hypocritical parry and thrust of awkward first-date conversations; all you really want to do is thrust."

"Intriguing," I said.

"Most people come around," the woman at the cash register said. She was eavesdropping.

Sib continued. "Now you have the ability to avoid that wasteful social dance, to exchange those banal soul-sucking conversations about your day, with something much more pleasurable." He looked up. "This is where the dial-a-feel settings come in." He cleared his throat again. "Rotate the dial three notches to the left and feel the oily clasp of a . . ."

"Oily clasp?" That didn't sound good at all.

"That's what it says." Sib chewed at his lower lip.

"What can I help you with, guys?" Playtime was over, the woman at the cash register was now standing beside us.

I didn't want Sib to ask her about the Dial-a-feel, so I got right down to business. "I was interested in an inflatable sheep."

"Oh, we don't sell those anymore." The announcement was accompanied by a finger flutter.

"Really? A friend of mine had one delivered to his house a couple of days ago. It was in a box with your logo."

The woman scrunched up her face. A Dial-An-Emotion device might describe the expression as the puzzled exasperation of a struggling small businesswoman. "It's been more than a year since I sold the last one in stock. Supply chain issues. They were manufactured in Germany, and we couldn't get replacement gas cartridges anymore."

"Hmmm." Now that I thought of it, you wouldn't want that vinyl sheep staring at you after using it. You'd want to deflate it and hide it away in a bag, within a box, inside a closet. You could always re-inflate it the next time you felt the urge but were too busy to interact with real barnyard animals.

"It's not cost effective as a one-use novelty-balloon," the woman said.

"Novelty?"

"Oh, the balloons weren't sex toys. They were supposed to be decorations for outdoor parties."

"Ah." Sib and I shuffled uncomfortably, disabled by the woman's candor.

"The one I saw had ... um ... these holes ..."

"That's just a gimmick," the woman said, "something to giggle over."

"Oh."

"Would you guys like to see anything on a live model?"

"You have live models?" I glanced at the mannequins to see if any of them was breathing.

"I have *a* live model. Singular." The woman laughed in a disarming way. "The outfits look completely different when they're swishing around." Her fingers did a little air-dance.

There was a door behind the cash register. Maybe a live model was lurking there, waiting for the opportunity to parade around, mostly naked, in front of two strangers. In a way, I was curious about who might pop out of that door. Ormond's a small city, so it might well be someone I knew from High School.

Then again, I *didn't* want to see who was behind the door because Ormond is a small city, and it might well be someone I knew from High School. And there were lots of other psychological inhibitors at play. When Sib and I went to strip bars, we always made fun of the middle-aged, toothless city workers who hogged the first row, right next to the stage; we considered their behavior pathetic. It would be hard to maintain that superior attitude if we made some woman strut through the crowded aisles of this little store. Plus, I had a deeply rooted, working-class reluctance to waste someone's time. There was no way I was going to buy frilly lingerie. I didn't have a girlfriend to give it to, and it would feel too weird to buy crotchless underwear in the hopes that I someday would. Anyway, I already felt guilty about staring at Ilene in the restaurant every day, and I didn't want to slip any further down that slope that would probably end in a Dial-A-Feel purchase.

"No thanks," I said, "I was really just interested in the sheep."

"Because our friend had one," Sib added.

"Okay." The woman didn't seem inordinately disappointed.

Next to Ewe

We walked out the door and encountered a throng of public-school-aged kids. Of course, I assumed they were here to gawk at the provocative mannequins, but that was wrong. The crowd was assembled to watch feeding time at the serpentarium next door.

A young woman in that establishment was centering a large glass cube in the window, so the kids outside could easily see. She flipped a door down at the front of the cube and an enormous snakehead slowly emerged from the container, its tongue tasting the air. The snake seemed to know it was feeding time.

The young woman was holding a pair of steel tongs in her hand. She reached into a fiber-board box and pulled out a guinea pig by its tail. The little animal lifted its head to check out the audience.

The snake's initial movement was too quick to see, but the kids on the sidewalk all flinched at the same time as the guinea pig disappeared.

"Jesus," Sib said, "It's like watching you eat pancakes."

He had a point. I tend to loop arms around my plate, ready to fend off competitors and barely take time to chew. I think it's part of that working-class package of attitudes where food looms inordinately large in your life, even if you aren't actually starving.

The young woman inside the serpentarium wheeled

that glass container out of the way and replaced it with a smaller aquarium. This time I could see a label: Eastern Green Mamba. The young woman placed a live mouse in the aquarium. The mouse walked around its new home, completely unaware that a bright green head was slowly tracking it. The little mammal stood up on its hind legs, facing the store window and twitched his nose.

"Boom!" one of the kids said, as the Mamba struck.

"He's a heat seeker," another kid informed us. Clearly, they were regulars on feeding day.

"That snake looks a little like Fahmi," I said. Sib's uncle always wore bright green ties and his eyes never seemed to blink. Whenever I saw Fahmi, he gave me a version of the hard-working-immigrant spiel, but I think his success had more to do with snake-like ruthlessness.

The mamba was wheeled away and replaced by a much smaller, pure white "Albino Corn Snake."

This reptile was lifted out of its cage, and immediately curled around the young woman's left wrist. The animal delicately plucked a cricket from the woman's right palm.

"That one's like yours," one of the kids said to a friend.

"Yeah."

I guess the free show eventually led to snake purchases. These kids would be experienced, predatory consumers when they graduated to watching the live model next door.

When we were back in the Blazer, Sib asked why I didn't want to see a live lingerie model. "What would it hurt?"

"My dignity."

"That's rich, after the shit I've seen you pull the past two days. You don't have any dignity."

He was almost right, but I felt compelled to insist "I've got a tiny scrap left." But that scrap was probably smaller than the cricket singing "When you Wish upon a Star" in an Albino Corn Snake's stomach.

Chapter five

Coyotes really like tongue

On Friday, it was Tamara's turn to babysit the smoke shop. I stopped by to get a newspaper, but also to see how she was doing after the dognapping. Tamara had Blaise in the store with her and that meant one of two things. Either she had a strong emotional need to be near the little guy, or she didn't trust Karsci to take proper care of him at home.

I wondered if Tamara had reason to worry about her husband's loyalty. She lifted Blaise up onto the counter so he could supervise when I paid for the newspaper.

Of course, while I was leaning against the counter and chatting, I was thinking about the furry red scrap of lingerie that was hanging in the woman's closet. I felt terrible, but I couldn't turn that nonsense off. Blaise knew what I was up to and made huffing noises of disapproval.

"He needs a bathroom break," Tamara said.

I took Blaise's leash and walked him out the back door of our plaza alcove. The dog sniffed and peed, sniffed and peed. In all, he deposited a teaspoon of liquid on a dozen different car tires.

When I returned Blaise to the smoke shop, Tamara looked relieved, as if she had just barely survived the separation. Blaise lay down for a nap in a doggie bed near his owner's feet.

I didn't want to distress Tamara, but I felt I had to ask a couple of follow-up questions about the dognapping. I suspected that Blaise's safe return wasn't the end of the story, it was just a warmup for another act, yet to come. "Have you had any strange phone calls at your house lately, maybe someone hanging up immediately after you answer the phone?"

Tamara shook her head. "No. Why do you ask?"

"I thought someone might still be monitoring your schedules, charting when you're home and when you're away."

"Do you think Blaise is still in danger?"

"Would you pay another ransom?" The dognapping

wasn't quite so ridiculous if it was a successful template for a series of crimes.

Tamara's chin dropped down to her chest. "Yes," she admitted sadly. "But we've already taken precautions. Karsci changed all the locks and we've got a better light in the backyard."

I nodded. Naturally, they would be on guard for the short term, but they would be at a disadvantage in any type of waiting game. I thought about the PhD thesis Sib read in the library, the document that described a hundred dognappings a month in Chicago. Maybe the criminals didn't plan to re-steal Blaise over and over, maybe they had five or six new-Blaises lined up. But what I suspected, deep down, was that Blaise was just a trial run for a completely different crime.

Would someone who paid two thousand dollars for a dog pay twenty thousand, or fifty thousand, for a human? It was a reasonable assumption.

"I want to talk to that retired typing teacher, the guy with a beagle, that Karsci mentioned. I'd like to know if he saw anything suspicious over the last couple of weeks." Dog walkers are creatures of habit and notice small changes along their routes. "When does Mr. Bourne make his rounds?"

"Oh, I never see him. It's only Karsci that bumps into him. It must be early in the morning, just before seven, because that's when he takes Blaise out."

I nodded. "I'll drive there early tomorrow morning and see if we can't accidentally meet."

But the next morning presented a conflict. I had a meeting with a bank manager who was trying to do two jobs at once and failing miserably. He'd bought a small motel, just eight units, and was using his secretary at the bank to make bookings, which was bound to eventually implode because banks like to have the undivided attention of their employees. The manager had also loaned himself a considerable amount of money to renovate the motel units but had stiffed the roofers and carpet installers.

I met the bank manager in the parking lot of his motel and asked him, point blank, if he wanted me to burn the place down so he could collect insurance. He said he would consider it and let me know but wasn't sure if his policy would pay the true replacement cost or a steeply depreciated amount. Essentially, the banker gave the impression he would love to jettison all of his stress and take a nap underneath his desk.

The irony of this meeting wasn't lost on me, *I* was a person struggling to do two jobs at once, unsure if I was primarily an albino corn snake or a cricket.

Anyway, ten minutes after we said goodbye, I delivered a Radio Shack recording of that conversation to the proprietor of the roofing company who was getting jerked around. He would either use the tape to extort his money from the manager, or just get a measure of satisfaction by playing the tape to the man's regional supervisor and having the banker fired.

Some people harbor a surprising amount of animus towards people who have wronged them. It doesn't matter if you're talking about roofing contractors or librarians, some people are violently protective of their perceived status.

At any rate, the meeting with the motel manager/banker was a command performance and I had to temporarily hang my detective aspirations in the closet like a piece of furry lingerie.

I ended up sitting in Miele's alone that afternoon, because Sib was making up for lost time at his store. I was eating a clubhouse, glancing at the newspaper, and trying to camouflage my fascination with Ilene's torso movements.

BIZARRE HUNTING TRAGEDY

The headline was on the front page, lower left corner, sharing the main stage with a continent-wide gas shortage and a cabinet shuffle.

The hunting-accident story included a photograph of an elderly man holding a shotgun with one hand and using his other to point into a scrubby patch of bush. A beagle was standing between his legs. The dog's smiling face was turned towards the camera. I started to read.

Henry Bourne was taking his beagle for a walk last evening when he found a disarticulated and partially decomposed body.

I recognized that name. He was the Polat's neighbor, the guy Karsci occasionally met when he was walking Blaise. He was the person I'd planned to interview before my sleazy paralegal duties got in the way.

Mr. Bourne explained that he always carried a gun on his walks because there were aggressive coyotes in the area, and he wanted to protect Snoopy. That's right, his beagle was named Snoopy. I immediately thought the coyote excuse was bullshit because Karsci had said his neighbour liked to hunt birds. The man probably had to concoct an excuse for carrying a weapon within the city's boundaries.

Anyway, Snoopy had bounded across a patch of grass and when Henry followed, he found a brown Ford pickup truck tucked into a stand of poplars . . . and a messy corpse.

The body had been ripped apart by scavengers, and its clothing had been shredded, but police were able to find a bullet hole in a scrap of cloth. A .22 rifle was a few yards away from the body, and the surrounding meadow was full of coyote pawprints.

Thomas

Okay, maybe Henry Bourne wasn't full of shit.

The article went on a brief editorial tangent about draconian hunting restrictions and the ecological value of a coyote "cull."

Then, the bombshell: there was a strange "decoy" in the vicinity of the hunter's corpse. Police speculated that the hunter used the decoy to attract coyotes, but attracted another poacher instead, and was shot by accident. The police suggested that the shooter had left the scene without fully realizing what had happened.

I thought that was very clever. The shooter was being offered up a plausible excuse so he might decide to do the right thing and turn himself in. Once the hunter was safely in custody, the "accident" theory might change.

The article graciously pointed out that Mr. Bourne's weapon was a shotgun loaded with pellets, but the body he discovered had been shot with a single bullet. He was being publicly excluded as a suspect.

The article said it was impossible to determine exactly when the victim was shot because the body was so badly damaged, but the incident probably occurred last weekend. The victim's identity wasn't released because next of kin hadn't been located by press time.

Mr. Bourne said that hunters frequently visit the area to shoot deer, pheasant, grouse, and coyote. Mr.

Bourne also said he noticed a Chevy Blazer driving back and forth in the area last Friday and assumed it was one of those hunters. He hadn't seen the vehicle since.

Holy shit, *I* was a suspect! For some strange reason, I found that oddly amusing. Guess I won't be driving near Mr. Bourne's neck of the woods in My Blazer, after all.

I flipped to page two for my favourite feature: "What Was That Siren?" The column listed every police, fire and ambulance call since the last issue. The discovery of the half-eaten body was mentioned, right at the top of the list, courtesy of the sensational nature of the incident, but there was no additional information.

The column right beside "What Was That Siren?" was a community promotional piece called "In Ormond." Basically, it listed bake sales, car washes, and penny raffles. I usually didn't pay much attention to it, but today there was an extremely interesting item: Friday Fish Fry!!!!!!!! At the Hunters and Anglers Club.

It was time to become a real private investigator, again.

I left the paper behind for the next lucky customer and walked to Sib's clothing store. I didn't actually enter until I was sure that Fahmi wasn't around. Sib's uncle always creeped me out.

"Hey."

Thomas

"Hey." Sib waved at me then sold some old lady a *third* sweater. It always amazed me that Sib could be such a great salesman and still have to spend his Friday nights with people like me. His charm seemed to be reserved for paying customers.

I waited for the lady to cash out then said, "we've got to swap vehicles."

"Okay." Sib liked the Blazer. We flipped our keys through the air to make the exchange.

"I've got an errand to run, but I don't want the guy to recognize my vehicle."

"Sure. What's on for later this evening?"

"A special treat. We're going to eat fish and chips at the Hunting and Fishing Club."

I drove to the fire-lane near Karsci's house, planning to knock on Henry Bourne's door, show him my freshly printed private investigator's card, and ask him for more information about the body he found. Obviously, I was interested to learn if the "decoy" mentioned in the newspaper article was an inflatable sheep.

I met Henry (and Snoopy) on route, they were standing by a field marked off with orange police tape. I pulled over and parked Sib's Grenada on a soft gravel shoulder. It was a new model from Ford, and it was okay, but for what he paid for it, it should have looked a lot less like a Grenada. Mr. Bourne stared at me. Snoopy positioned himself between his owner's legs and stared, as well.

"Mr. Bourne . . ." I walked across the road and handed him the card Maggie had printed for me.

He looked at it and said, "aren't you supposed to have a badge?"

"No. We're not allowed to have badges. Private investigators aren't supposed to use any identification that might make people believe they are official police." I made that up, off the cuff, but it turns out it was accurate. The Department of Corrections has all kinds of rules governing rental detectives, and I would eventually break almost all of them. But that day, I accidentally stated something that was true.

"That makes sense." Bourne nodded and seemed impressed by my honesty. He returned the card.

I figured I might as well suck up some more. "Is it alright if I pet your dog?"

"Sure." Mr. Bourne took a step backwards, exposing the animal.

I bent down and scratched the loose skin on the animal's forehead. Snoopy smiled as only beagles and homeless people can, then licked my hand. I stood up and volunteered some more information. "One of your neighbors . . ." I gestured towards Karsci's house ". . .

had his dog kidnapped last week."

"Blaise?" It was a suspiciously good guess but, then again, he only had one neighbour. "My God, that's terrible."

"The dog was returned, but I still don't know who was responsible for taking him. I'd like to find out who it was, so no other dogs get harmed." I thought it would help to insinuate that Snoopy was in potential danger.

"Oh, sure, anything I can do to help."

"You didn't recognize the person you found in the bush, yesterday, did you?"

"Son, his own mother wouldn't recognize him. The coyotes ate his *face*." He shook his head. "*That* didn't get reported in the paper." Then his eyes narrowed. "Do you think he had something to do with kidnapping Blaise?"

"I just figured that if he was a stranger, he might be a suspect. Dognapping's a surprisingly big problem. Over one hundred dogs are kidnapped every month in the city of Chicago alone." Why learn a fact if you aren't going to trot it out in a pretentious way. "The person responsible might very well be a professional pet-napper. If that's the case, he would have to stake out the Polat's house and learn when the little dog would be vulnerable." I found myself carefully enunciating words. I wanted to be the most conscientious phony private investigator possible.

Next to Ewe

"Oh, the guy was a stranger alright."

The confident declaration surprised me. "How do you know that?" I wondered if Mr. Bourne had gone through the victim's wallet before he phoned police.

"His vehicle had Saskatchewan plates." Mr. Bourne shuffled his feet, like a primary school student who was about to confess he had shot the spitball. He squirmed for a few seconds, then said "the dead man's name was Mitch Jayne. An officer asked me if I recognized it. I'm not really supposed to tell anyone else, until police track down next of kin."

I thanked him, and said I didn't know anyone with that name, but I would respect his confidence.

"Son, did you read that article in the paper, today?"

"Yes."

"Well, a lot of it was hogwash."

"Yes?" I wasn't judgmental.

"I said that Snoopy ran into the bush and found the body, but that wasn't true. I waded in there to check out the truck, myself. I'd seen it parked there for days, and I was curious. On my way over, I tripped on the corpse. I went down and sunk my knee into what was left of his head. I messed it up bad. The police were nice though, they didn't publicize anything that would make me look bad. They made sure the reporters knew my gun couldn't have done the damage."

Thomas

"The article said something about a 'decoy.' What kind of animal was it?"

Mr. Bourne sniffed. "If it was a decoy, it was the stupidest one I've ever heard of. The police told me it was an inflatable sheep."

Bingo.

"Did you see it?"

"No. Someone had shot the thing, so it was just a scrap of rubber in the grass over there." He pointed to the edge of the little field.

"You don't think an inflatable decoy would work?"

"Decoys are supposed to have the silhouette of an animal. A puffy balloon wouldn't look natural, and it would smell funny. Most likely, it would scare predators away."

"Maybe it moves in the breeze and rustles the grass around. It could be the movement that attracts the predator, not the shape of the balloon." I'd read a story where hunters attracted migrating flocks of geese by scattering rags in a field. And I once caught a seven-pound bass using a top water lure that looked like a kitchen magician. I didn't see why decoys had to be ultra-realistic.

"Well . . ." Mr. Bourne scratched his cheek with the gun stock. "You might have something, there."

"Walk me through this. Where was the man lying?"

Next to Ewe

"Come on, I'll show you." He ducked underneath the orange police tape. "The detective said they were finished with the crime scene. We can walk wherever we want."

We stopped where the grass had been flattened by a hundred footsteps. "The body was right here."

I looked but couldn't see any blood on the grass. I guess the man had stopped bleeding long before the coyotes ripped him apart.

"The rubber sheep was over here." We walked twenty yards towards the lake. Mr. Bourne pointed at a little orange flag stuck in the ground. It must have been an evidence marker.

Of course, I couldn't ask Mr. Bourne if he happened to stick his arm in the sheep and extract a wad of hundred-dollar bills. The dognapping story was my entre into this conversation but now, I wanted to drop the connection like grade ten French. I didn't want Mr. Bourne phoning the cops and leading them to Karsci. He was still a client, in a way, and I wanted to respect his wishes about not involving the police, especially if the skeleton in his closet was wearing furry red lingerie.

"Hey," Mr. Bourne said, "do you think the killer took the man's arms so he couldn't be identified? So, he wouldn't have fingerprints?"

I managed to keep a straight face. "Did the police

find a wallet on him?"

"Yeah," Mr. Bourne admitted, sadly.

"It wouldn't make much sense to take the guy's arms but leave the wallet."

"Yeah, I guess. You have to admit it's weird, though. All the body parts that could be used to identify the guy are missing: teeth and fingertips." Mr. Bourne had another epiphany. "Maybe the identity in the wallet isn't accurate! Maybe the wallet was left there to deliberately mislead everyone."

Yeah. Maybe the coyotes planted the inflatable sheep, hoping to attract a careless hunter. I just nodded and said, "deep waters."

Snoopy sniffed around in the grass and occasionally raised his head as if he had an inclination to join our conversation.

"Did the police think the victim was a hunter?"

Mr. Bourne nodded. "They figured the .22 lying near him must be his gun. It wouldn't make any sense for the shooter to leave a gun behind."

"The article said the man was killed with a bullet not buckshot. Well, how would they know that, if the body was so damaged?"

"From the hole in his coat. One of the officers told me that."

I tried to re-cap the situation. "So, there were two

hunters here, on opposite sides of the inflatable sheep. One guy fires, the bullet rips through the sheep, hits the other hunter, and he drops." I was moving my arms like a community theater director blocking out a scene. Before the grass got trampled, it was probably waist high and there was a slight hump in the ground near the ex-sheep. But an *accident* still didn't seem likely. "The guy who pulled the trigger *must* have known he hit someone."

Mr. Bourne stuck out his lower lip and nodded.

"But the two men couldn't have been part of the same hunting party," I said. "The shooter wouldn't have left his buddy here to bleed out."

"Mmmmmmm." Mr. Bourne wasn't sure about that. "They might have been hunting together, but that didn't necessarily mean they liked each other."

That was a variation on what I was thinking. The two men may have kidnapped a dog together and retrieved the ransom from a rubber sheep together, but that didn't necessarily mean they were friends. Maybe there was a slight disagreement about how to divide the spoils.

We stood there for quite a while without saying anything. Snoopy broke the trance with a very soft whine. His nose was pointed towards the lake and one paw was raised slightly in the air. "Well, I'd best be going," Mr. Bourne said. Snoopy's behavior must have meant that their favorite game was lurking nearby. "I hope you figure out who took Blaise." The beagle was on the move, its head and back flat as a board, and Mr. Bourne jogged after him.

I climbed into Sib's Grenada and waited for a few minutes. Sure enough, there was a gunshot and several pheasants exploded into the air.

Coyotes, my ass.

I drove the Blazer to the Hunters and Anglers Club, figuring a truck would help us blend in. Sib was worried about what to wear, but I couldn't imagine there was a secret dress code.

The Club was outside the western fringe of the city, a half hour's drive. It wasn't terribly far from the Polat's house, as the pheasant flies. I filled Sib in on my visit to the scene of the 'hunting accident.' He agreed that we shouldn't tell police about the dognapping connection yet. He was eager to play detective a little longer.

"How old is Karsci?" I asked. Sib paid a lot more attention to our circle of acquaintances than I did.

"He's forty-one." The answer was quick and confident, as I suspected it would be.

"How do you know?"

"Well, last year, Tamara was trying to organize that

fortieth birthday party for him."

"That's right." She had floated the idea with some of her regular customers and some of the tenants in the plaza.

"And, at the time, she mentioned she was exactly ten years younger than him. Their birthdays are within a week."

"That was last summer, in July," I said.

"Yes. So, Karsci turned forty-one and Tamara turned thirty-one *this* July." Sib had pivoted neatly to Tamara. Her age was important, in a way, based on a shared, juvenile assumption that it was impolite to fantasize about a friend's wife if she wasn't age appropriate. Anyway, we'd dissected women in our conversations so often, curiosity about Tamara's age didn't seem intrusive or unusual.

The birthday party ended up being cancelled at the last minute because Karsci freaked out when his wife told him the good news. Apparently, he's ultra-sensitive about aging. Tamara tried to be nonchalant about it, but we could tell she was embarrassed. No one likes to admit they don't know a partner as well as they thought.

We crossed the railroad tracks then veered left down a poorly graded gravel road towards the escarpment. A portable sign with interchangeable letters said "Fish Fry Ahead—Five Bones Adults, Three Bones Kids." A minute later we saw The Hunting and Fishing Club which was within casting distance of the train tracks. The long front drive was a causeway bisecting a small, excavated lake, dividing it into two separate pools. A sign with the word "Trout" pointed left and a sign with the word "Bass" pointed right. Several hills loomed behind the building, probably formed with the material removed when the ponds were created. The parking area was a gravel pad between the artificial lakes and a sprawling ranch-style building.

Several dozen vehicles, about half of them trucks, were lined up like arrestees awaiting a pat down, noses pointed toward a block wall. There was no visible door.

As we exited the Blazer there was a blast of gunfire that came from the opposite side of the building. Sib and I looked at each other. There was another disconcerting blast. "Well, it *is* a gun club," he said. We walked, tentatively, to the north end of the building and encountered a handprinted placard. "Danger. If this sign is on the pathway, turn around, we're shooting skeet. Only enter range from building (Blue door by bar)"

We walked to the south end of the building and found another entrance.

Sib pulled the door open, and stepped to the side so I could take the first bullet.

"Oh, hello there." Surprisingly, we were greeted by

a familiar voice. A woman was sitting at a table selling the fish fry tickets. She was wearing a low-cut camo-patterned tank top. It took me a few seconds to recognize her as the proprietor of the Ero-Teek Bo-Teek, the person who had generously offered to have an employee parade in front of us, nearly naked. "Thanks for coming," she said, "the fish dinners are our biggest fundraiser."

"You're a hunter?" Sib asked.

"Target shooter." She cocked her index finger, lined up Sib's heart and pulled the trigger. Her imaginary gun recoiled, then she blew across the barrel. Sib twitched as if a lipstick-stained bullet had found the mark.

The fish dinner fundraisers would soon have competition from an inflatable sheep hunt if Mrs. Ionides had her way.

"Is the fish from your ponds?" Sib asked.

The Ero-Teek lady laughed. "No, it's pickerel from Lake Erie."

I paid for the dinners and the lady spoke into a microphone. "Two more, number forty-one and forty-two." Her voice echoed far away within a kitchen, and there was another blast of gunfire from the skeet range. She gave us our tickets and we walked inside. There was a bar at one end of a large open room and the central area was filled with folding wooden tables. Sib went to the bar and got us two Blackhorse beers. We wandered around the room looking at portraits of hunting dogs and reading posters about local hunting regulations.

Mrs. Ionides, the librarian, waved at us from a distant table.

It wasn't long before an amplified voice shouted, "Forty-one and Forty-two" and there was another blast of gunfire. We picked up our dinners at the bar while several people entered via the blue door, carrying shotguns. We sat down at an empty table.

I didn't really have a plan of action, beyond extending my streak of not using the stove in my apartment. I wanted to find out if any hunt club members had floated the idea of a floating, treasure-filled pinata. But I'm not particularly good at initiating small talk. I decided I would count how many beers Mrs. Ionides drank and approach her if she staggered noticeably on the way to the washroom.

Not much of a plan.

The fish dinners were pretty good, and the scoop of coleslaw was a nice surprise. I was used to the creamy tub of goo that came with Kentucky Fried Chicken, and the Hunt Club's version actually looked like real vegetable matter.

But Sib and I were soon treated to a much bigger surprise. The Club ran out of fish at dinner number fifty, so the lady from the Ero-Teek Bo-Teek was able to leave her post at the door, and she sat down at our table. When I thought about it, it made sense because we were the only people under fifty years of age and that made the three of us natural cohorts.

"Are you guys thinking of becoming members?"

"I've got a Walther PPK," I said. "I wouldn't mind learning how to shoot properly."

"Cool. Where'd you get the Walther?"

"My grandfather picked it up during the war." My paralegal life had turned me into a fluent liar.

"There's an indoor range in the basement, but I like the outdoors one a lot better. They set up solid body targets." Then the woman formally introduced herself and I had to bite the insides of my cheeks to keep from laughing. Her name was Lacey DeValera. She sold sexy underwear, and her name was Lacey.

Sib bumped my knee under the table, so he was thinking the same thing. I wished he wasn't so immature.

Lacey suddenly got up from the table and I wondered if she was offended by the suppressed giggles. But she came back in less than a minute with three beer necks between the knuckles of her left hand.

I couldn't remember the last time a woman bought me a beer.

My greatest investigative skill when tracking deadbeat tenants has always been to locate the drunkest neighbor and encourage that person to talk. It was a pretty good technique because, at that time, people drank a lot more than they do today, and drunks always liked to talk. There wasn't much societal push-back, either. Even drinking and driving was effectively decriminalized because sympathetic policemen were just as juvenile, repressed, and unhappy as everyone else, and coped by drinking just as much as everyone else.

I figured I may as well reprise the drunken-interview technique here at the Hunt Club.

Sib and I crawled into the pail, like we did most Fridays, and Lacey climbed right in with us. We took turns buying Blackhorse until the bartender ran out, then we switched to Bohemian Maid. Sib emigrated from London when he was a kid, but he always reacquired the British accent when he was drunk and talking to a woman. So, when he went to the bar, he always made sure to ask Lacey "whot wudyuz like?" and she smiled in approval.

But she gave me equal treatment by saying she liked my name, Davin. Apparently, she was of Irish decent, too.

"How did you end up becoming a member in a gun club?" I asked. In 1970's Canada, people didn't give each other Glocks for Christmas.

"Oh, my girlfriend is a member, so she invited me

along one Sunday to shoot."

Sib was tapping morse code against my knee again. I knew the message was a frenzied question: what did the word "girlfriend" mean? Did it refer to a hunting buddy or someone who received gifts of furry lingerie?

"But I've always liked guns. My mom once gave me a Glock for Christmas."

It ends up that Lacey was born on an army base in Germany and grew up immersed in gun culture. We talked a lot about hunting, and thinking back, that was probably to avoid talking about lingerie.

I'm using "lingerie" as a code word for any honest discussion about sex. That sort of thing could only end in an exploration of why I was damaged and lonely. No one needs that.

"Do people ever use decoys for hunting, around here?" I asked.

"Not that I've heard." Lacey wiped her mouth with the back of her hand. "People here complain about the local *conservation officers* using deer decoys to trick people into shooting from their truck windows. They've even got a decoy that moves its head to the side, as if the animal has seen you. Apparently, that's the trigger. People think the animal is going to bound away forever and they can't resist blasting." She took another sloppy pull from her bottle. "Then the officer pops out of the bushes and issues a ticket."

"Isn't that entrapment?" Sib scratched his ear with the neck of a beer bottle. Entrapment had been in the news a lot lately in drug trafficking prosecutions.

"Nah. Because the person isn't being *lured* into something he wasn't going to do, anyway." She gave the word *lured* a comical emphasis, because the booze was starting to play games with her tongue. "*Lured*," she said again, and laughed. "If you're driving down the road with your window open and a gun in your lap you haven't been *lured*."

"*Lured*," Sib repeated. I knew he would soon start talking about his clothing store, trying to give Lacey the impression that he was a better-looking version of his rich uncle Fahmi. I didn't like it when he did that, because there was no possible way I could keep up. I just couldn't make my grimy paralegal business sound glamorous. I had ripped up too many piss-stained carpets.

"Are there many hunting accidents in this area?" I asked. Sib tapped away at my knee again. This time the message meant, "quit talking about the stupid dognapping case and focus on the slim possibility that this woman is *luring* us."

I ignored him.

"One old guy . . ." Lacey twisted around in her seat

to look for him and indicated the proper target with a nod of her head. "That old guy in the red shirt." The person happened to be sitting near Mrs. Ionides. "You see how his head looks funny?"

The skin on his bald dome was streaked with white and pink scars.

"He's a fruit farmer and he *says* his head got damaged while he was trying to repair a bird-banger." Those noise makers, designed to keep blackbirds away from grape crops, were armed with blank shotgun shells. "He *says* he accidentally activated the device while he was inspecting the bell." I guess the bangers had megaphone-like openings to magnify the noise. Lacey leaned forward to mime the action and Sib and I stared down the little crevice in her camo tank top. "But I heard that his brother-in-law shot him while they were hunting pheasant out of season."

"Do you think it was deliberate?"

"Hmmmm." Lacey leaned back and I made a monumental effort not to stare at her breasts. "It's hard to say. Farmland can be really valuable now that housing developments are popping up all over the place, and there was some issue about an inheritance. They say that money is the root of all evil."

"I guess I'll never be evil," I said, trying to give the impression that I was a principled person who floated above crass materialism like an Ero-Teek sheep.

Lacey reached over and touched the back of my hand.

Sib was tapping at my knee. This time the message was a desperate "pass the puck, pass the puck, pass the puck." I wanted to tell him to relax. The only time we had ever managed to con a girl into having sex with both of us, we got a killer case of crabs. Despite what we might read in *Letters to Penthouse* columns, the world wasn't full of women desperate to sleep with a sweater salesman and a corporate bagman.

"Do you happen to know Mrs. Ionides?" I asked. I tilted my head sloppily towards the table with the wounded farmer. Now that Lacey had pointed it out, the guy's head was really grotesque. The bird-banger (or brother-law) really let him have it at close range.

Lacey's hand was back on top of my knuckles.

"The librarian? Yeah, she's part of the fundraising committee, just like me."

"I met her at the library the other day and she was talking about shooting floating pinatas as some sort of fundraiser."

"Oh yeah." A fingernail started lightly playing with a lump on the back of my hand. It was a healed-over break from an old smoke-hole fight in high school.

PassthepuckPassthepuckPassthepuck!!!!!!!

"She made that proposal at our meeting just the other day, but it was a no-go, for obvious safety reasons. Someone suggested tethering the balloons, but Shelly didn't like that, she wanted people to climb in their trucks and chase the thing, cross country, wherever it blew."

I asked Lacey about the BIZARRE HUNTING ACCIDENT reported in the paper, if anyone in the club had dropped any suspicious hints that they knew more about the incident than the paper reported. Unfortunately, my brain was distracted by another series of knee taps. This time it was Lacey banging out a morse code message and I imagined it was: ditch your asshole friend, ditch your asshole friend, ditch your asshole friend.

I twisted around and slapped Sib on the shoulder. His elbow slipped off the table and his face hit the surface, hard.

"Ooooh." Lacey came over to our side and shifted him back into his chair. Then she went to the bar and got a bag of ice.

"Thanks," Sib said.

I vaguely remember saying that I would take Sib home and Lacey promising to follow us in her green 1970 Caprice. I think she was planning to hook up with me after I tucked my friend into bed, but I wasn't absolutely certain. We weren't the least bit concerned about the dangers of unleashing our vehicles like untethered sheep balloons and letting them roam all over public roadways. It seems unconscionable, now, but at the time we thought it was perfectly reasonable.

I was highly motivated to get rid of Sib then make out in the back seat of a green Chevy Caprice with a white landau roof. It's funny, but Lacey's car was starting to play a huge part in that little fantasy.

But actualizing the dream wasn't going to be easy. First of all, I had to negotiate the causeway between two giant fishponds. Driving in to the Hunting and Fishing Club, the water seemed picturesque, but now it was just a cruel joke. I wondered how many members had been fished out of the drink after closing time. The next obstacle was the level Railway crossing. I was so eager to proceed with operation corkscrew that I almost drove around the barrier in order to dump Sib quicker. Of course, that would have been a false economy if we had been flattened by a locomotive or we had *lured* Lacey to follow us, and she had been flattened by a locomotive.

The third obstacle was a deer grazing on the side of the road. It was an enormous buck and its eyes flashed yellow in the Blazer's headlights. It raised its head and looked at us. I wondered if it was a conservation-officer decoy, and I almost left the road to see if it would leap out of the way. Lacey was honking behind us and pointing at the animal through her open window.

I had decided to dump Sib on the couch at my apartment. It was too risky getting him into his own place, in his parents' house. It had a separate entrance, but Mr. Akram might still come to the front door with his robe flapping and bitch me out for corrupting his son, which would be a half-truth.

We were almost home when we encountered the most significant obstacle, a police car with flashing lights.

Somehow, I understood that the officer was waving me in to the parking lot of a United Church and, equally amazing, I decided not to tromp on the gas and try to escape. The Blazer would have stalled and sent me a note of apology.

Lacey briefly stopped on the road shoulder and shouted, "I'll see you later," through the open passenger window, then roared into the night.

The officer watched her disappear then looked at my face, and seemed to instantly read the entire story, right up to the depressing ending. "Get out of the car, sir." The "sir" was only slightly sarcastic, and the entire request was tinged with sympathy. I opened the door, let one foot touch the gravel and almost collapsed.

"Woah, hang on" the officer said, "you shouldn't be

driving."

"I know," I said, "but I was highly motivated." I glanced at the ghost of the Caprice, which was still lingering on the road shoulder.

I pulled out my wallet and showed him my driver's license.

He looked at the address. "You just live over there." We could see my building, crouching like a giant deer just beyond a stand of London Plane trees. I thought the cop was going to suggest parking the Silverado and walking the rest of the way. He obviously understood the loss of girl and Caprice.

"Why didn't you get Slick, here, to drive." He gestured at Sib, who always managed to look good, even after barfing. "He's straight as a pin."

"Okay." I was going to have to start calling Sib Slick, myself.

"Switch seats, and I'll follow you there."

"Okay. Thanks." Like I said, this happened prior to a massive policy shift. Sib and I had been stopped eighteen times (nineteen now) when we were staggering drunk and had only received one citation for a defective horn. I lurched around to the passenger side and Shoved Sib behind the wheel. He managed to turn the key and smile at the officer. But really, his body was like a deflated sheep, a pile of useless rubber.

While the officer walked back to his cruiser, I reached over with my left foot, tromped on the brake and shifted into drive. Then I carefully activated the turn signal and steered us back onto the road using only my left hand. Sib turned towards me and smiled; his lips flecked with beer foam and saliva.

It was a tough couple of blocks because I didn't want to look like I was crawling into Sib's lap but the slight shift in perspective from the passenger side was weird. I was flirting with the ditch, but I didn't dare over-correct and cross the centerline. I managed to make the right-hand turn into my parking area and stop before the Blazer crawled through my living room window. I got out of the truck and pretended that Sib was supporting *me* as we clumped to the entrance.

"I'm going to come back to check that you stay put," the officer shouted through an open window.

I lifted Sib's arm up in a wave and shouted "thanks."

Chapter six

Got to get next to ewe

I thought I might get Sib to help me with the dognapping case on Saturday morning, because he didn't have to go into his store until 1:00 pm, but he was absolutely useless. I set the alarm and positioned it about an inch from his left ear, then left the basement.

The plan was to go to the library, but I had to swing by the Ero-Teek Bo-Teek first. If I didn't make a decent attempt to establish a dysfunctional relationship with Lacey, I would never forgive myself. A sign posted on the door said that they didn't open until 2:00pm on Saturday. I guess people who buy Dial-A-Feel machines aren't early risers. I jammed my newest business card into the plastic frame, so the corner stuck up like a deer head in the bush. I wrote a little note on it saying I wasn't really a private detective, but I would still like to see her. I resisted the impulse to decorate the note with a bubbly heart.

Business first.

I stopped at a corner store to buy a hangover special, a foot-long cold cut sub with a three-egg omelet poured on top. It's my go-to morning-after meal. It took me less than three minutes to eat, then I was ready to face my only paralegal business task of the day.

As I said before, Ormond is a small city, and the library has a copy of every high school yearbook. Surprisingly, those books have been useful investigative tools whenever I have to track down a deadbeat tenant. I admit, that doesn't happen very often because landlords are usually happy to let the memory of bad tenants dissipate like wet carpet smells. But occasionally, someone crawls under a property manager's skin, and they are determined to sue or prosecute. That's when they pay me to find the person.

If the person didn't leave a forwarding address and alcoholic neighbors don't know where he worked, I'll leaf through the age-appropriate sections of the yearbooks looking for the name. Today's deadbeats were often flamboyant characters when they were in high school and got a disproportionate amount of ink in the yearbook. They usually appeared in lots of candid "buddy" pictures, or team photos and, generally, had lots of acquaintances who might know where they moved.

Maggie Haberman typically gives me a stack of city directories, and even lets me use the library phone to call the deadbeat's potential friends. I almost always get a hit within five calls.

My most obnoxious deadbeats are home-grown.

I often tell people I'm part of the high school reunion committee trying to start a computer database and I've encountered a stale address for **insert dip-shit's name here**. The high school reunion pitch mentioned alongside new technology works pretty well.

That Saturday morning, I got a solid lead ("he's in some high rise by the new mall") on call number three, thanked Maggie and went to the area. There were three high-rises by the new mall, and **insert name** wasn't on any of the tenant directories. But, since he was new, his name may not have been added to the list yet, or maybe he had used a phony name on his rental application. I needed to talk to the superintendents about their new move-ins. I decided to start with the middle apartment. It was sort of like my strategy leaving the Hunting and Fishing Club last night, where I picked the middle road of the three that I saw between the fish ponds.

I buzzed the super, asked about **insert**, and was immediately given a unit number. He had used his real name; it just hadn't been added to the lobby list yet.

I was done. I didn't have to confront the deadbeat, that pleasure was reserved for an angry property manager. I just went back to my plaza office and typed up an invoice.

I couldn't call my phone service to ask for messages, yet. I desperately wanted Lacey DeValera to respond to the note I left on her door. If she didn't, if the phone service just had the usual list of property management contacts, I would likely contemplate a dramatic suicide. I would rub peanut butter on my private parts, jump into the dumpster behind the rear plaza doors and let the rats end it all.

I needed to wait until two o'clock so Lacey would have a chance to see my card.

I went by the smoke shop to say hello to Tamara. Blaise was there as well, nestled into his doggie bed. Tamara asked me if I read the article in the paper about the "hunting" accident.

I said I had.

She nodded and said, "thank God, that's over with."

Tamara clearly thought that the dead body was associated with Blaise's dognapping, even though the sheep hadn't been specifically mentioned.

But that man's death clearly didn't mean the threat was "over." If one dog-napper shot a partner, it meant one extremely violent criminal was still at large. But I didn't want to distress Tamara unnecessarily. She asked me if I could take Blaise outside to pee. I grabbed his leash, and we went out the back door. This time I counted as Blaise marked nine separate car tires, including the Blazer. The dog had amazing bladder control, and a deep hatred for steel-belted rubber.

I returned Blaise, then went into the pet food store that shared our end of the plaza alcove. A lady at the grooming station recognized me as a fellow tenant and recent dog-walker. "I heard about Blaise," she said, shaking her head.

"He's had a tough time," I replied. "I want to get the little guy a treat."

"He likes these." She walked to a rack of mummified pig ears.

They looked disgusting, but I bought a couple. "Who would do something like that?" the woman said as she rang in the purchase.

It could be someone like *you*, I thought, someone who knew that the Polats had an expensive dog and an open wallet when it came to his welfare. But I quoted the PhD thesis Sib had read in the library last week. "There are over a hundred dognappings every month in Chicago alone."

"No!"

"People are still stealing dogs and selling them to Universities for psychology experiments." I remembered that from Dr. Singer's radio interview. He had talked about electrified metal floor grids as a form of behavior modification. I'm not sure what those experiments were intended to prove.

"People steal dogs for experiments?"

"Apparently."

"No!"

"It's a crazy world."

"It certainly is."

I wondered what Dr. Singer thought about feeding captive guinea pigs, mice, and crickets to captive snakes.

Maybe it was time to stop thinking.

It was certainly time to change the subject. "That's one easy-going dog," I said, pointing to a border Collie that was napping while a groomer shaved badly matted hair from its butt. There were days where Sib and I could have used a similar service, but I didn't say that out loud.

"Oh, we had to sedate Hunter," the lady whispered. Maybe she was afraid Hunter would overhear.

"What would someone do if a pet owner wanted to trim a dog like Hunter at home? Do you sell sedatives?"

"Well, a vet has to prescribe them, but we do sell tranquillizers."

I nodded and was about to leave with my mummified pigs' ears when the woman volunteered some information. "Karsci uses trazadone to trim Blaise's nails."

Really.

You shouldn't own paranoia if you aren't going to let it run around in the yard from time to time. I remembered Karsci telling me that Tamara always groomed and trimmed Blaise, but the pet store lady implied *he* was the one doing those chores. Once again, I suspected that the smoke shop owner wasn't being completely honest with me.

I delivered the pigs' ears and Blaise smiled like my dad when someone bought him a beer.

Then, I went back to the library and arranged a call to the librarian at Farewell Creek-Tecumseh Saskatchewan. The Polats had some measure of communication with someone from that town, based on the return address scrap I had seen attached to their fridge. The disarticulated body discovered by Henry Bourne, had once driven a truck with Saskatchewan plates.

My opinions about the dognapping were shifting like a sheep balloon in the swirling winds of circumstance. But my most durable theory was that the criminal knew the Polats intimately. That acquaintance *could* have been formed in another province.

Karsci often talked about his escape from Kurdistan, but it always sounded like he was a much younger man at the time. He had only been a tenant in my plaza for three years, and now he was forty-one, according to Sib. Sometimes new immigrants get shipped to tiny, rural corners of the country before they are able to relocate in more urban areas. Maybe Karsci walked through Farewell Creek-Tecumseh Saskatchewan on his way to Southern Ontario. Maybe he'd traded rifle-butt stories with a recently deceased man named Mitch Jayne.

Maggie Haberman logged me onto the reference department's long-distance line. The library paid about half the civilian rate and those savings could be passed along to a valued customer who frequently returned stolen books.

The Saskatchewan librarian was eager to help me out, which was surprising. Maybe people on the prairies were too busy discing their fields to sign out books. But her assistance wasn't completely free, I had to tell her why I was calling and that meant giving a pretty thorough description of the dognapping. Then the woman surprised me by saying she would look in the local high school yearbook for "Jaynes" because she recalled the family name. She was taking a page from my investigative playbook, and that made me feel better about my own amateur sleuth instincts.

She promised to send a fax to Ms. Haberman within a day or two.

With nothing left to do at the library, I went back to my little office, steeled myself, and called the phone service to retrieve my messages. There were three calls from property management firms who contracted out really unpleasant files to independents like me. There was a message from Sib, who said he couldn't hang around with me tonight because he had a date. "She's a nuuuuuuuuuuurse," the receptionist said, with her usual business-monotone.

"What?"

"I wasn't the one who took the message, but that's the way it's written: nuuuuuuuuuuurse. I guess the guy must be excited to be dating a nurse." The receptionist made a "humph" sound. I don't remember getting editorial comment with any of my previous ten thousand messages.

I tried to imagine what happened. Sib must have gone into work, (somehow) wrangled a date with one of his customers, then immediately bragged about it through my phone service. Sib ran a menswear store, but most of his customers were women so, theoretically, there was lots of opportunity. But Fahmi would be pissed off if he caught Sib treating his job like a dating service and, anyway, Sib's self-confidence was generally too fragile for anything but sweater-talk.

The nurse/customer must have done all the heavy lifting.

I couldn't help myself. "Are nurses supposed to be exciting?" To me, anyone in a uniform was exciting, but I needed a female opinion.

"I wouldn't know," the woman said, "maybe your friend gets turned on by white shoes." She sounded indignant.

"My friend sells clothing," I said by way of explanation. "He really does consider shoes to be the windows of the soul."

The receptionist was lost in her own thoughts. "People have weird ideas about nurses. They seem to think that they can . . ." She suddenly stopped talking, and I was disappointed because it sounded like she was on the cusp of parroting some juvenile urban myth that I would have appreciated, like nurses use their specialized medical knowledge to unlock hidden pleasure zones.

There was a loud sigh. "Do you want the rest of your messages?" the receptionist asked.

"Yes please."

"Lacey asks you to stop by the store at 6:00pm."

Thomas

There were four more property management tasks, but I had to ask the receptionist to repeat them, twice. After hearing Lacey's message, my brain was like a bicycle chain that slipped off its sprocket, got tangled in a pant cuff, then was cut into pieces, and welded into the shape of a heart.

You don't know how empty your life is until a phone message thrills you to the core. Suddenly, throwing someone's stained mattresses and chipped night tables down a flight of exterior stairs no longer seemed fulfilling. A woman wanted to see me—after seeing me—after talking to me, after drinking me under the table and watching me get pulled over by a cop. She couldn't plead ignorance about my character; the interest must be somewhat sincere.

Dear Penthouse: I always used to look at your readers' mail column and laugh at the fantasies concocted by your pathetic letter-writers. For years, I've thought of them as a group of sad, disaffected half-wits who only had "Dial-a-Feel Pleasure Devices" to inform their sad delusions about human interaction. What reasonable person could believe that a vivacious, big-busted bombshell would actually lust for those shaky, fumbling fingers to unbutton her perfectly starched nurse's uniform and throw her into a laundry hamper for six minutes of unbridled pleasure? Yes, I used to think that your letters were shallow fabrications until, one day, I wandered into my local lingerie boutique . . .

While I drove back to my apartment, Junior Johnson came on the radio and sang "I've gotta get next to ewe." This time, the lyrics seemed inspirational, like I really *was* approaching a destination, not just spinning my wheels on a country road. Junior understood that it was an important night for me.

The Blazer seemed to understand it was an important evening, as well, and was on its best behavior. When I stepped on the gas it immediately accelerated, without sighing first, and the windshield washers sprayed extra fluid on the glass.

When I pushed the door of the Ero-Teek Bo-Teek open, I could barely make it across the threshold. I stood there with my knuckles dragging and lower lip quivering, staring at the displays of crotchless panties and spanking tools. Lacey left the counter and walked over to me as if we were standing in the reference department of the library, ready to do a homework assignment.

She placed both hands on my chest and reached up to kiss me on the cheek. It was a natural movement, as if we had known each other for years, a simple act of affection that I had never witnessed in my parents.

"Let's go out and eat," she said, "I'm starving."

Lacey had arranged to be dropped off at the boutique, somehow knowing I would pick her up. Her faith was touching. Obviously, I was motivated to show up, I was like a deer snuffling around a feeding station. But she couldn't be absolutely sure that my truck hadn't been impounded in the traffic stop.

"Did you get arrested?" Lacey asked as we walked in front of the serpentarium.

"No. The officer just gave us a stern warning to leave the vehicle parked." She held my hand and glanced into the serpentarium window, before separating to climb into the passenger side of the Blazer.

"I think I recognized the cop," she said.

"Traffic stop?" I experienced a brief, jealous fantasy about the cop composing his own Letter to Penthouse after pulling over a woman who owned a lingerie business.

"No. He came to the store last Valentine's Day."

"What did he buy?" I was mildly curious about the cop, but I also wondered if Lacey had an eidetic memory for her customers, like Sib did.

Lacey bit her upper lip. "A fairly conventional Teddy."

I can't remember which restaurant we went to. I

only remember the thrill I got when we accidentally brushed legs under the table. Of course, I was completely mistaken and was flirting with the table pedestal. It took me a lot longer than it should have to figure that out.

Lacey suggested visiting my apartment afterwards, saving me a lot of mental agony.

There may or may not have been sex. At that time, people were weirdly strategic about using the word. But there certainly was sexual *activity* and it was absolutely clear that I might soon write an actual Letter to Penthouse unless I fumbled the ball, badly.

We lay on my bed after fooling around, and Lacey told me about her "live model." That was a strange topic of conversation, but I have to admit I appreciated it. The model was a drama student at Strathroy, and she was willing to strut around in lingerie, for the minimum wage, to develop stage presence. I guess, the idea was that she couldn't possibly be self-conscious on stage after modeling slutty lingerie to strangers. The woman also posed naked for a high school figure drawing class, and that news almost gave me a heart-attack. When I got expelled from Lord Elgin, I only made a half-hearted attempt to get re-enrolled. If there was a live nude art class model—and Lacey said she was "gorgeous"—I would have clawed my way through the bricks.

Lacey also found my copy of *Buf Swinger*, on her

way to the washroom, which might have been embarrassing. "BUF" was an acronym for "Big Up Front" and was shockingly juvenile. I found it on one of my eviction/clean-up jobs and was fascinated by the lame, niche sexuality. Basically, it was just reams of breast photos. I really didn't understand fetishes, even though my own creepy behavior might suggest I probably should.

Thankfully, Lacey didn't make any sarcastic comments about the skin rag, she just flipped through the pages until she found her store's mail-order ad and showed it to me. Apparently, her furry bra merchandise and miscellaneous toys were just a tease, her biggest sellers were a set of camo-patterned bras and briefs—which she was currently wearing—and novelty panties like the one with Felix the Cat's face on them. Mail orders generated more than three quarters of her income.

Try to guess her most lucrative sales period.

You might think it would be the weeks preceding Valentine's Day or Christmas. No! It was the weekend before July fourth, American Independence Day. For some reason, Americans seem to associate liberty with crotchless panties and "self-help" puppets.

"Hey, have you ever used Speedy Delivery for local orders?" I asked. I had to know if Lacey was even peripherally involved with the dognapping. I couldn't bear the thought that she might be hooking up with me as part of an operational safety assessment.

"I did," Lacey said. "But I couldn't coordinate the deliveries to make it cost effective. Eventually I switched everything to Canada Post Express."

I'd spent almost ten years listening to deadbeat tenants and I was like a machine fine-tuned to perceive deflection, equivocation and fabrication. There was none of that in Lacey's voice, her words were like silver dollars dropping onto a church collection plate.

Weird as it may sound, Lacey was at her most erotic when she talked business statistics. She mentioned that three quarters of her customers were men. I wasn't really surprised since she had a live model available. But it was also counter-intuitive, since most of the clothing was designed for women. I told her that Sib's *Mens*wear store had a strongly female clientele. Lacey agreed that the retail world was a backwards place, at times.

I ended up telling Lacey all about the dognapping, including the detail of the ransom stuffed in one of her discontinued sheep balloons. Real private investigators probably didn't spill their guts after sticking a hand into some camo-patterned underwear but, then again, I'm not a real private investigator. Lacey listened without making any smart-assed comments and seemed genuinely concerned about the little dog's psychological welfare.

I told her that I was embarrassed and worried by a brewing suspicion that my friend Karsci had conspired to kidnap his own wife's pet.

Of course, the accusation didn't make strict logical sense. If Karsci was upset that the dog was expensive, why stuff two thousand dollars into a vinyl sheep, just to get the pet returned? Even if the dog was killed, there was no guarantee that the financial bleeding would stop. There was nothing stopping Tamara from immediately buying a more expensive replacement. So, I had eventually modified my misgivings and decided that Karsci was responding to pressure exerted by a murky past.

Lacey tried to make sense of my rambling account. "So, you think someone from Farewell Creek. . ."

"Farewell Creek-Tecumseh, Saskatchewan. . ."

". . . Saskatchewan, blackmailed him for two thousand dollars, and he had to come up with the stupid dognap plan so his wife wouldn't know where the money was going?"

I nodded and Lacey felt the movement because her fingertips happened to be resting on my face. "Does his wife control the purse strings?"

"I don't think so," I admitted. "Karsci spends more hours at the store, but Tamara works on the books. It feels like a reasonably equal partnership." I sighed and suddenly felt discouraged. Printing the words "Private Investigations" on a business card didn't magically make the assertion real. "Ah . . . It's all horseshit."

"No, it's not horseshit," Lacey said, "you've just grabbed the wrong end of the shovel."

I suddenly felt extremely tired. My body hadn't fully recovered from last night's bender.

"Sequi pecuniam," Lacey said as I fell asleep.

The next morning, we went to breakfast at Miele's and I was surprised that the world's most beautiful waitress, Ilene, was working. Usually, she was Tuesday to Saturday and Janine took care of the pretend-to-go-to-church crowd.

"Hey!" Ilene said to Lacey.

"Hey." Clearly the two women recognized each other and, naturally I started imagining that Ilene was wearing Felix the cat panties under her apron. It was disconcerting, and I began to wish that my brain stem would hurry through its protracted and painful puberty.

We ordered breakfast specials and Ilene seemed more inclined to hang around and refill coffee cups now that it was Lacey sitting with me rather than Sib. I always suspected that Sib was dragging me down.

Speak of the devil.

Thomas

Sib came into Miele's and slid into the booth with us, which I thought was presumptuous. But Lacey didn't seem offended, so I didn't accidentally spill coffee on his lap.

"I heard you had a date last night," Lacey said to him. I must have mentioned it, although I can't imagine any point in our date or make-out session where it would have been appropriate.

"Yeah." Sib smiled so hard it made *my* jaw hurt.

"So, when I leave, are you guys going to compare notes?"

"No." Sib was horrified. "If you talk about it, you jinx it, everybody knows that."

"Good answer," Lacey nodded.

Sib and I had been talking about women as if they were items in a lingerie catalogue for so long, I wasn't sure I could stop. But if anything could change my behavior, it was a superstitious belief that talking about a good thing would automatically end it.

Somehow, we got onto the topic of Lacey's model developing stage presence through sleazy underwear. When Ilene hipped into the conversation, we had a fairly serious debate. Ilene said she admired the model's strategy. Sib surprised me by disagreeing. He didn't think it was necessary for the model/actress to have extreme self-confidence in order to be successful. Sib knew what he was talking about; he was a great salesman even though he was a well-dressed bag of insecurities. Then Ilene surprised me by softening her position a little. She mentioned that Glenn Hall used to throw up before every hockey game, even though he was one of the best goalies in the NHL. Hall was emotionally fragile but still won the Vezina trophy three times.

I could have offered myself up as a minor corroborating example. Every morning, I was one stained mattress away from leaping off an overpass into the windshield of a cement mixer, but I still slid into the same booth at Miele's, had a coffee, and ended up deciding things weren't all that bad. Who needed confidence?

Lacey seemed to be the arbiter of the debate. "What doesn't kill you, makes you stronger," she said.

"Sometimes, it warps you," I countered. I was thinking about Karsci walking out of Kurdistan with a rifle-butt dent in his head. Anyway, the guy who said "it makes you stronger" was Nietzsche and he died of syphilitic insanity hallucinating that his brains were running out of his nostrils. Apparently, a bout of pre-penicillin syphilis didn't make you stronger.

Wait a minute, the guy who died with brain matter flowing through his nose was Guy de Maupassant. My encyclopedia-reading was as spotty as some of the abandoned mattresses I dragged through apartment hallways.

Lacey paid for our breakfasts and Sib left Ilene a hundred percent tip.

Things were looking up.

I dropped Lacey off at her apartment, which was in an old Victorian mansion that had been carved into five separate living units. She invited me up to an interesting unit in the rear, which must have been servants' quarters back in the days when idiot elder sons diddled the chamber maids. The rooms were small but had high ceilings with plaster rosettes and carved crown moldings. I was fascinated from a sleazy business perspective. Most of my clients were upselling buildings just like this. The pitch was a classic case of misdirection where a verifiable—but meaningless—figure called a "gross income multiplier" was used to inflate the supposed value.

Lacey and I chatted for a few minutes, and I found out that her landlord was an elderly gentleman who had inherited the house from his elderly uncle, who was probably one of the people who diddled the chambermaids. I suggested that Lacey get her model to work on her stage presence with the guy and, in the meantime, negotiate a real estate deal. I knew an unprincipled broker who would lend me the mortgage money for a three-thousand-dollar fee and an exorbitant rate of return. It was outrageous but, at the time, a lot of short-term real-estate flips could absorb the screw-over.

Lacey knew her landlord well enough to broach the subject of a purchase, but I could tell she wasn't keen on the idea of immediately flipping the house, even for a big profit.

In a way, it was foolish for me to insert crass commercialism into a brand-new relationship. But I wasn't sure that incipient alcoholism and a used Blazer were enough to make me attractive in the long term, I was trying to upsell, like Sib did in his menswear store.

"I'll think about it." Lacey said. She kissed me and I walked down the stairs. I patted her Caprice on the hood on the way back to the Blazer. I wanted the car on my side if it were to chaperon us on our next date.

Earlier, during breakfast, somewhere between Glenn Hall throwing up and Lacey's model waxing her arms, I'd asked what "sequi pecuniam" meant. Lacey had whispered it while I was falling asleep and, considering my state of mind, it could have meant almost anything. It was Latin, so it might have indicated that Lacey was the embodiment of an ancient demon and we had just consummated a contract for possession of my soul. *The Exorcist* was a best seller at the time and it was common knowledge that all supernatural transactions were conducted in Latin.

It was a let-down to discover the phrase meant "follow the money."

Anyway, it gave me a focus for my next research assignment in the reference department at the public library. Maggie Haberman worked Sundays. The library was closed on Mondays and her day off was Tuesday. It's important to know people's schedules when your livelihood largely depends on favors.

The reference department had survey maps indicating the boundaries and ownership of farmland since the area was settled in the late 1700s. I'd used the old maps as the basis for fake property line and severance disputes for several of my clients. The newest sets of survey maps mocked out proposed housing developments on the fringes of the city.

If I was going to follow the money, I would have to start there.

Karsci's brand new house was the only building in a stalled subdivision. To me, that suggested he was more than just a resident, he was one of the developers. It was the guiding principle behind any 1970s real estate project: pay yourself first. It wouldn't surprise me if Karsci had assigned himself a lot, developed it, then run out of money before he could finish the rest of the project.

In that scenario, the dognapping might be a threat

from his own associates and investors, a subtle warning that Karsci had better pull his head out of his ass and frame a few more units to keep the step-payments flowing. I spread the maps all over the largest table, seriously inconveniencing a group of girls who were trying to do a school project on whale migration.

Of course, the newest maps weren't labeled with familiar founders' names like Culp, DeYonge, Merrit, or Coulter. Those old mill barons were gone, and Karsci's neighborhood was owned by Ontario Numbered Company 660073.

Interestingly enough, 660073 was one of my best customers when it came to fraudulent evictions. They owned or managed close to two thousand units in Ormond and Hamilton, including the plaza where Karsci and I rented space. They had also left three separate messages with my phone service yesterday.

I signed Maggie's phone log and called Ester, Ontario 660073's secretary. She should have been a partner; except she didn't drink enough and was the wrong gender. Ester never took a day off. In fact, Sunday was her most productive day because her pseudo-bosses weren't around. She answered the phone on the first ring as if I were the prom date she was waiting for.

"Hello Davin." I don't know how she did it, Ester always called me by name before I had a chance to say anything. Call Display may have been technically invented at that time, but it wouldn't be commonly available for more than a decade. I must make some sort of whistling noise with my nose every time I pick up a receiver. "What do you need?" Apparently, she could also read minds.

I recited the eleven-digit identification number I had copied from the city's development plan.

"What about it?" She recognized the project.

If I was talking to anyone else, I would have tried some feeble scam, like saying Karsci had hired me to represent him in the development deal. But Ester was out of my league. She was Glenn Hall after he had thrown up and I was the Zamboni driver's back up. She was impervious to my bullshit; I had no recourse but honesty. "Can you tell me if Karsci Polat has an ownership stake in that development?"

"Of course, I can't," Ester said. Then she snort-laughed. It was as close as she could come to making a joke. "But he doesn't." I didn't have to explain that Karsci was a tenant in one of her company's plazas, Ester's business knowledge was encyclopedic.

"Then why does he have that great house, right in the middle of the project?"

"He got a great deal because he paid cash. Dr. Braun used that money to pour the rest of the foundations on the street."

Dr. Braun was an obnoxious dental surgeon and key investor behind Ontario Numbered Company 660073. I did a lot of work for him and disliked him intensely. I also disliked his slutty second wife and his bratty son, Bernard.

"Why didn't the project get finished? Did Dr. Braun meet another future Mrs. Braun?" Sib and I sometimes saw Dr. Braun in a strip club called "The Jungle." He was a serial philanderer who couldn't keep his pants zipped.

"He's focusing on another project." Ester refused to be drawn in.

"But Karsci has *no* financial interest in the development where he lives?"

"No." Ester wasn't into small talk. She really didn't care why I wanted the information.

"Thank you."

"You're welcome." She was always scrupulously polite.

It's funny how my deviant thought processes had wrestled with the problem of Blaise's dognapping. Over the course of ten days, I had imagined that Blaise had been dispatched by angry neighbors, snatched by mad scientists, jettisoned by an owner because of his massive vet bills, exploited by criminals wanting to make a quick buck, exploited by criminals plotting a more heinous crime against the family, and—finally—part of a financial dispute amongst developers of an ineptly executed subdivision. I had suspected a delivery driver, a neighborhood dog walker, a librarian hunt club member, a lingerie saleswoman... yes, the appearance of the inflatable sheep in the drama had briefly made me wonder if my beautiful new girlfriend was involved.

"Mr. Chaney." Maggie called me by my last name whenever the area was full of grade eight girls.

"Yes?"

"I just got a package from the librarian in Farewell Creek-Tecumseh." Maggie held out a manilla envelope. I checked just to make sure it wasn't marked Speedy Delivery.

"Thank you," I said. Ester had taught me the importance of manners. Maggie started to gather up the development plan maps as the whale watchers gave me the stink eye.

"Here's your invoice." Maggie had the long-distance charges and next day delivery postage tallied up. I looked at the slip of paper: forty-seven dollars and eleven cents. That was a little more than my dad's take-home pay after a shift at the paper mill, but it was well worth it.

Chapter seven

I'm a curly-horned devil

I called Karsci and asked him to meet me at Miele's for a coffee. I figured I owed him a heads up.

He said "sure," immediately.

"Where's Tamara?" I asked him. I needed to get him alone.

"She took Blaise for a ride. I think they went down to the canal to chase geese." I heard him breathing like a French Bulldog. "Twenty-five minutes?"

"I'll be waiting."

I flopped into my regular booth, surprised to see Ilene working another Sunday shift. She slid a coffee under my nose, then started wrapping cutlery in napkins and stacking the little packages in a cabinet. It was one of the chores she did to avoid customers.

click—click—click

"Hey." Karsci waved and sidled towards the booth like he was going to ask me to dance. Ilene gave him a coffee then *click—click—click*

"What's up?" Karsci smiled around the rim of his cup.

I paused for a minute, working up the courage to answer honestly. "I know." We made wary eye contact and Karsci's cup was suddenly tethered to his lower lip. But his eyeballs tilted down as I pulled an envelope off my lap and placed it on the Formica.

"*What* do you know?" Karsci's cup broke from its mooring and moved ponderously down, touching the table like a dirigible landing in a field.

I pulled out a piece of paper, an eleven-by-seventeen-inch photocopied sheet from the Tecumseh Trappers yearbook and showed it to Karsci. He looked at the neat rows of faces from the graduating class and shrugged. I reached across the table and pointed to a face in the right-middle quadrant.

Karsci squinted and read the name: "Mitch Jayne." He looked up. "So what?"

"He's the guy who was shot in your neighborhood last week."

"Oh? He's the dead hunter they found on the fire-lane?"

"Yes, and look who's here." I pointed at a face in the bottom right quadrant.

Karsci's face darkened. "Alex Zahradnik."

"I thought you might recognize the surname. And look over here." My finger directed him to the left side of the sheet, the Trapper's grade eleven class.

"Tamara Zahradnik." I knew that Tamara was lying when she said she came from a little town in northern Ontario. She grew up in the hyphenated community of Farewell Creek-Tecumseh Saskatchewan.

"And here's her friend Deanna." The surname wasn't Lapierre, like on the envelope stuck to Karsci's fridge, because the woman wasn't married yet. Karsi nodded, however, so I had guessed right.

His future wife, his future wife's sibling, and the woman who sent them Christmas cards, were all classmates. They all went to the same small-town high school as Mitch Jayne, the guy who met a violent end in Ormond, next to an inflatable sheep with an extra hole.

Quite a coincidence.

"She must have worked it all out, previously," I said, "it's too complex for an impromptu performance."

Karsci took a drink of coffee, and tried to look like I hadn't just accused his wife of murder. "What do you mean?"

"I mean she bought two inflatable sheep a year ago. From a woman named Lacey DeValera, who has an amazing memory for customers. Tamara meant to use the sheep as balloon markers for your fortieth birthday party last summer. After you pulled the plug, she stored the sheep in the basement next to her hunting rifle."

"Hunting rifle?" Karsci shook his head. Ilene refilled our cups then moved slowly back to the cutlery station. *click—click—click* I waited, so Karsci had time to digest the information.

"Mitch Jayne was waiting for her in that field. Tamara drove down the fire-lane, and when she got close enough, she stuck the rifle out the driver's side window and shot Jayne like he was a giant gopher."

"Ground hog. Tamara used to shoot at a groundhog who lived underneath her family's porch."

"You're missing the point, bud."

"Why . . . why was she meeting him?"

"I assume Jayne was blackmailing her. I talked to a lady in Tecumseh, a librarian, who was familiar with the Zahradnik family history. Did you know that Tamara's stepfather was killed in a hunting accident?"

Karsci nodded weakly. "He shot at a coyote near their house. When he went to check the carcass, another hunter saw the movement in the grass and shot him, by mistake." There was a long pause, then Karsci added "it wasn't even a real coyote. Tamara's dad shot a decoy someone had placed there. No one was ever charged."

"Mrs. Adamovich . . ."

"Who the hell is that?" Karsci looked pained.

"She's the librarian. Mrs. Adamovich knows more about the people of Farewell Creek-Tecumseh than the census takers. I got the impression that Tamara's family was the center of a lot of gossip. Mrs. Adamovich said that Tamara's stepdad had an insurance policy and Tamara was the sole beneficiary, not her older stepbrother. Mrs. Adamovich told me the policy paid out something in the neighborhood of a hundred thousand dollars. I have no idea if that's . . ."

"She's right," Karsci said. "Tamara got a hundred thousand from her stepdad. That's the money that paid for our business . . . it paid for our house."

"Mrs. Adamovich told me that Tamara's stepbrother felt cheated."

Karsci leaned forward and his belly squeaked against the table. "Alex was an abusive jerk." Then, he repeated the word "ab-u-sive," drawing out each syllable, "in the most heinous way possible." He wanted to make sure I appreciated the sexual nature of the crime. "And her stepfather was *complicit*".

Word-A-Day strikes again.

"He knew all about it," Karsci growled, "the money was an attempt to make amends."

"I'm sympathetic," I said, "but your wife's behavior still scares me. Hey, maybe Mitch Jayne deserved to get shot. I'm assuming he threatened to tell his buddy, back in Saskatchewan, where a certain stepsister had relocated, and what her married name was. But look at the weird, unnecessary elaboration of the crime. She blasted an inflatable sheep to suggest Jayne's death was a messed-up hunting accident. That means the murder was premeditated." Technically, that elevated the crime to a hanging offense. No one in Canada had actually dangled since Ronald Turpin shot a policeman and went for a brief joy-ride in his cruiser, in 1962. But I was trying to make Tamara's situation sound as bleak as possible to break through Karsci's protective armor. "And that whole goofy dognapping story was concocted before she ever drove down the fire lane. More premeditation."

Karsci stared at the Formica and his nose twitched up and down. "Are you done?"

"Not nearly. She created the fuzzed-up ransom note in the public library and left copies on Shelly Ionides' desk, salting the library with evidence of a completely fictitious crime. I know she was in the library that day because that's when she signed out *Animal Liberation*." Maggie Haberman had showed me the "hot new arrivals" list with Tamara's signature. Karsci chewed his coffee. "At best, her behavior is insane." I wanted Karsci to start mulling over that possible defense strategy, so I repeated the word: "insane."

In fact, based on what Karsci just intimated about the sexual abuse, I could easily imagine a lawyer characterizing the shooting as a delayed psychotic episode, perhaps entwining revenge with a subconscious re-enactment of her stepfather's death.

But I was also starting to wonder if Tamara was the one who fired into that moving patch of grass back in Farewell Creek-Tecumseh, then added the coyote decoy and rifle after the fact, to disguise an execution as a hunting accident. Maybe, in Ormond, Tamara was subconsciously re-enacting her father's *murder*. The night we were waiting for Blaise's dog-nappers, Tamara told the story about cruising home late at night and firing a rifle at her porch.

Maybe, she'd actually gotten a couple of those groundhogs she was proxy-hunting.

Of course, if Tamara wanted revenge and retribution, she should have shot her ab-u-sive stepbrother rather than her stepfather or a high school acquaintance, but sometimes people blame enablers more than the actual criminals.

"The dognapping story *wasn't* crazy." Karsci felt

compelled to defend his wife. "It worked."

"Jesus, Karsci, it *didn't* work. *I* figured out what happened, and I'm a colossal screw-up. All it took was ten days and forty-seven dollars and eleven cents in long distance charges." I was exaggerating Tamara's peril. The police seemed happy enough to label a stranger's death an "accident." And although I was inordinately proud of uncovering the truth, I had, as Lacey said, repeatedly grabbed the wrong end of the shovel then tripped over it. It was unlikely that anyone else could follow those footsteps. Even when I fully appreciated that the dognapping was an inside job, I pegged the wrong insider. Like generations of people before me, I was eager to blame the immigrant.

"Karsci, you've got to think this through. Tamara must have drugged Blaise and hid him in the attic office, while you guys were running around pretending to look for him. She had to drug *you*, so you'd take a nap on the couch while she was fake dognapping him and planting the note. Presumably Jayne was already lying dead in the grass, next to one shredded sheep. Then we go through that whole rigmarole with sheep number two, and she has to knock you out *again* so she can deliver Blaise to the plaza and leash him to my door handle."

I'd accused Karsci of lying to me several times over the past couple of weeks, but I realized, now, that he was actually a prisoner of the truth. He didn't angrily deny what I said or claim responsibility himself to shield his wife. He stoically accepted the fact that Tamara had orchestrated the scheme behind his back. At some point he figured out what had really happened, or maybe Tamara confessed. All he could do now, however, was make the best of a bad situation, put lipstick on a rubber sheep.

"It was Tamara's idea to ask you for help," Karsci said. Maybe he thought that mitigated his wife's behavior but, to me, that detail made her seem even more devious.

"Blaise must have been in the attic office all day, Friday. He was there when I poked my nose over the threshold and looked around." When I mentally replayed the incident I heard faint, raspy breathing, but that was probably guilty editing. "Think about how dangerous it is to pump a small animal full of trazadone so it's comatose for sixteen hours. She might have killed Blaise herself. You've mentioned that the little guy has respiratory problems, he might have stopped breathing. . ." Maybe Tamara would have gone so far as to deliver the corpse to herself, via Speedy Delivery, and blame it on the dog-nappers, but I didn't want to say that. "You better sleep with one eye open, bud."

"Tamara would never hurt me."

Thomas

I sighed deeply. "Listen, Tamara obviously dropped her rifle at the scene, after she shot the guy, otherwise the police would never think it was a hunting accident." Canada didn't have its long gun registry at the time, so there was no documentation that could connect an ancient hunting rifle to any specific person. In a way, it was quite clever to leave the gun behind. But "clever" isn't always genetically spliced with "harmless."

"Tamara might have a second gun." I held up two fingers so Karsci could follow my reasoning. "She seems to like things in pairs. She had two floating sheep." I waggled the fingers. "She certainly had two distinct life-narratives. For all you know, there's another weapon hidden behind the nightstand where she keeps the trazadone. One day, she may decide that you're just another gopher who needs to be shot."

"Groundhog," Karsci mumbled. Then "Tamara would never hurt me." When people start to repeat themselves it's a sure sign the argument is winding down.

But I tried to appeal to Karsci's empathetic side. "Tamara might not hurt you, but what about me? I'm the biggest threat in her life right now, assuming her stepbrother still doesn't know where she is. I don't want to have panic attacks every time a car approaches me from behind, wondering if the window is rolled down, and there's a rifle poking out."

"She would never hurt you, either. Blaise likes you and that means you're okay."

Great, I had the endorsement of a wheezy French bulldog. "What if Blaise decides to bark at me one day?"

Karsci grimaced. "I'm not explaining myself very well." Stress ramped up the accent slightly. It wasn't quite Boris Badenov, but it was approaching Pavel Chekov from Star Trek. "Tamara likes *you*; she respects *you*, that's why she insisted I ask for your help."

"She just wanted a witness to the bogus dog-napping."

"No." Karsci squirmed, and his expression tightened. "Listen, what are you worried about? You can take care of yourself. You've got your gun with you."

"Sure, I do," I lied, as I patted my waistband, just underneath the table. I'd been pushing Karsci pretty hard, and I didn't want him to crack and opportunistically take me out because I was as helpless as a groundhog. "But I'm not on guard every minute of the day."

click—click—click

We sat there, staring at each other, pretending that there was some sort of solution within reach and Ilene pretended not to listen to us pretending. *click—click—click*

Thomas

That was the best-stocked cutlery cabinet in the universe.

"I'll talk to her," Karsci said finally. He heaved his bulk out of the booth.

My second meeting with Karsci, the following evening, after the smoke shop closed, was surreal.

"Listen," he said to me, "it would be hypocritical to talk about someone else being damaged." He lightly touched the rifle-butt mark above his ear. "We're all damaged."

We sat in the same booth at Miele's and he started out by asking me if I had my gun. This time, I showed him the butt of a toy that was tucked in my waistband. I didn't want to carry the Walther in case Karsci tipped-off police and had me arrested, just to be a dick. But I didn't want him to think I was vulnerable, either.

"I appreciate your honesty," he said, "Tamara and I both appreciate it, and I wanted you to know that."

I nodded. "Since we're being so honest with each other, I'd like you to explain something to me."

"Okay," Karsci was non-committal.

"If Tamara had to shoot the guy, okay, she had to shoot him. But why not just hide the body? Why leave him beside a wounded inflatable sheep in that field? Why make up that whole batshit-crazy story about the dognapping?"

Karsci wasn't offended by my question. He spoke slowly and patiently, as if *I* was the one who had been clubbed in the head with a Russian rifle butt. "The Police think it was a hunting accident. They're satisfied." He shrugged. "If Tamara hid the body, that couldn't have happened. She would have to worry about the body staying hidden, hoping coyotes didn't dig it up and drag a femur onto Mr. Bourne's lawn. And with a hunting accident, she didn't have to figure out what to do with the guy's truck."

I hated to admit it but mentioning Jayne's truck made Tamara's staging of the scene seem less ridiculous. She couldn't drive two vehicles.

"But the sheep . . ."

"She got the idea when we were on vacation, five or six years ago. We were driving through Tennessee and when we were in Oakridge, she heard a radio station contest. The DJs put Flying Burrito Brothers tickets in an inflatable sheep and released it. People phoned in all weekend to report sightings. The DJs would interrupt songs to notify listeners about the latest location. You see, whoever shot the sheep, got to retrieve the tickets, that was the prize." Karsci mimed the retrieval action with his giant hands, and I felt sorry for the sheep, even though it was vinyl and over-priced.

Thomas

I didn't know how to respond. I kind of liked The Flying Burrito Brothers, and I was sad that they were peripherally involved in that nonsense.

"Three teams of sheep hunters came together, just outside of Frozen Head Park, near Petros." Karsci moved his hands through the air to mime the convergence. "Someone winged the sheep when it was a half mile high, but two people shot each other, trying to finish it off when it fluttered near the ground."

"Frozen Head?"

"One of the Cumberland mountains has a snowy peak." There was a long pause and Karsci shuffled his feet. "You can't make this shit up," he said. "None of the sheep hunters were charged. It was considered an accident, pure and simple." He looked up at me with a weak smile. "You can see the similarity."

I felt sorry for Karsci because he was fighting so hard to make his wife's bizarre choices sound logical and reasonable. I suppose no one wanted to admit that a life partner, someone who was willing to wear red furry lingerie, was an unbalanced murderer.

Later, I got Maggie Haberman to make a research request from the Knoxville public library and she was sent copies of several microfiche articles describing the ill-fated radio promotion and subsequent bloodbath. The Tennessee floating sheep story was true.

Incidentally, The Flying Burrito Brothers cancelled their show after hearing about the fiasco. They were the only ones who acted with any dignity.

"Tamara didn't do anything wrong." Karsci delivered the moral to his story as forcefully as he could. "Her stepbrother was an abusive jerk." His head lowered and he did the same verbal trick, elongating the word "abusive" so I would understand he wasn't talking about normal sibling teasing. "He certainly didn't deserve any of the insurance money. And that blackmailer, Jayne..." Karsci shrugged, "he's just a human heart worm. The world's a better place without him."

I scratched at my cheek. "What if the police do a ballistics examination on the bullet that killed Jayne? They'll see it was fired from the rifle lying in the grass beside him, and the hunting accident story will fall apart."

Karsci smiled. "The dognapping was a *fail-safe*." The unusual term must have been another entry in Karsci's word-a-day calendar. Despite the stressful circumstance, he enjoyed using it. "If the hunting story didn't work, we would tell the police about Blaise, and say we were scared to come forward, because one of the dog-nappers was still at large, and he was a killer."

And I would corroborate their bullshit.

When he left Miele's, Karsci stuck out his big mitt

and shook my vinyl hoof. "I want to thank you," he said. "We *both* thank you."

I hoped he was talking about himself and Tamara, not Blaise.

Like I said, the meeting was surreal because we talked as if things had been settled when, in reality, circumstances were still floating above our heads. I hadn't made any commitment to keep quiet about the crime, and Karsci hadn't made any dependable assurance of my safety. I tapped the toy gun in my waistband and felt like an idiot.

I wasn't even sure what I expected to gain from a meeting with Karsci. Did I think Tamara would give herself up after I privately exposed her as the shooter? My thoughts must have been leaning that way because I was making little suggestions about her possible defense strategy. But legal rights and wrongs didn't mean much to me after so many years of delivering fraudulent eviction notices. You can have the law on your side and still be a weasel.

To be perfectly honest, talking to Karsci was largely ego-stroking, I didn't want the Polats thinking I could be manipulated like an ovine balloon.

Meanwhile, like Junior Johnson says, even a Cadillac will sometimes spin its wheels. My daily paralegal tasks would continue, I'd deliver eviction notices to tenants who wouldn't know that I was once a brilliant detective.

Rinse and repeat. Wipe your hands on the curtains and move on.

The next day, I parked beside the dumpsters and noticed there was a white Audi in Karsci's usual spot. The plaza wasn't open yet, so I had to unlock the rear door. I didn't have to disarm an alarm system because the plaza wouldn't have one for another decade.

"Harf." The sound was a wheezy exhalation of air.

Blaise was tied to the door handle of my little office again. I unhooked his leash and walked a couple of steps towards the smoke shop. Two strangers were rearranging the skin mags in their racks. Part of my brain was happy to see that *Buf Swinger* was moving up in the world, the latest issue now positioned on the top shelf between *Hustler* and *Swank*.

"Hello," I said, and the couple turned around, smiling. In retail, you have to treat everyone like a potential customer. I introduced myself as the paralegal next door while Blaise rolled and unrolled his tongue. There was a lot of handshaking and petting.

"Where's Karsci?" He hadn't taken a day off in the three years I'd known him. The Tennessee vacation he talked about happened well before they opened the smoke shop.

"Oh, the sale finally went through," Mrs. Bozkurt

said, "we're the new owners."

"Ah," I nodded as if I knew a transaction was imminent. The word "finally" was interesting, it indicated that a deal was in the works even before Blaise was (supposedly) dognapped. Maybe Tamara was aware of Mitch Jayne's presence in the city and had tried her best to avoid a violent confrontation, by selling out and leaving. "Can I be your first customer?" I pulled a morning paper out of a bundle that hadn't been shelved yet. It cost a quarter, but I also snapped a dollar bill a couple of times and asked them to keep the bill for good luck.

Mrs. Bozkurt beamed and gave me a pen to sign it. She said she would frame the dollar and hang it behind the cash register. "I wrote GOOD LUCK FROM YOUR FRIENDS DAVIN AND BLAISE." The little dog huffed as if he were following along and approved of the sentiment.

I went back to my office, picked up the coffee cup that Sib used whenever he came to visit, and filled it with water so Blaise could have a drink. Then I took him out back so he could pee on some car tires.

I sat down at my desk and pretended that folding and re-folding a newspaper was legitimate work. Blaise lay down in the alcove between my feet. I sipped at a coffee, read portions of a dozen articles, then turned to my favorite feature: "What was that Siren?" I always left it for last, like dessert.

Today, there were twenty-seven brief entries on the list, but buried within the usual sadness and idiocy was a fascinating, extended explanation of an ambulance call. A balloon had drifted over The Pirate's Cove Family Campground and a rumor rapidly circulated that it was full of money. Campers believed it had blown across the lake from Toronto and contained a promotional prize from a radio station.

So, several campers pursued the object in trucks and on motorcycles and they actually shot it down near Rockway, after an eight-mile chase. The campers kept firing at the balloon even as it rapidly descended. "I wanted to have the kill shot," one man explained, "that would give me dibs on what was inside." Two people were wounded, one seriously, in the crossfire.

The balloon was shaped like a sheep, and the paper even mentioned that it was "anatomically correct." But the disappointed hunters didn't find money hidden in any of its nooks and crannies. The newspaper suggested that the campers had been misled by an urban myth.

That was a reasonable assumption.

Even before legions of idiots populated the future-internet, there were outlandish stories circulating through the city's bingo halls, and trailer parks. For example, some farmers persistently believed that a giant black puma was killing livestock near Caisterville, and other people claimed to have seen a shark fin prowling the shoreline of Lake Ontario. I've personally overheard several morons in Miele's claiming that the snot-nosed guy begging for nickels in the market square is actually a millionaire who takes a limousine home to a mansion every evening. Now a floating sheep balloon full of money was part of that proud tradition.

I assumed that a few of the hunters were members of the local Club, and they had heard Mrs. Ionides talk about Blaise's ransom-delivery.

"Charges are *not* expected to be filed," the little article concluded and there was no connection made to an earlier hunting accident where Mitch Jayne's disarticulated corpse was found near a shredded sheep balloon.

As I have already mentioned, Tamara knew the value of a nickel, and she wasn't going to jettison two thousand dollars, especially when the money was absolutely irrelevant to her plan. I thought about the evening we spent waiting for the vinyl sheep to be delivered. I replayed the tape in my head several times and saw Tamara clutch the roll of bills, insert her hand into the sheep, then twist her back to me with the effort of withdrawing her fist. I heard the sound of a small helium gas cannister clicking off her rings.

I didn't suspect anything at the time, but it was obvious in hindsight, that the money was never left inside the sheep. Tamara had cleverly removed the roll as she violently yanked her arm out.

The realization made me smile.

That Friday must have been a stressful evening for Tamara. She had shot a blackmailer from a moving car window, and initiated a complex, phony dognapping narrative. She would have been pretty confident that Karsci would believe her story 1) because he truly loved her, and 2) his brain had been shirred by Ero-Teek lingerie.

But when *I* kept harping about the ridiculous ransom retrieval scheme, it must have made her wonder about the solidity of her sandcastles. Still, Tamara managed to deflect my paranoia and convince me that her anguish was solely related to Blaise's welfare . . . while palming the two thousand dollars.

"What was that, Siren?" was a reminder to be on guard against arrogance, that everyone's hoof shall slide in due time. I was wrong to assume that a treasure hunt involving a rubber sheep was doomed to fail. I now had two examples of the technique (kind of) working. Theoretically, at least, the floating sheep could be retrieved. The fact that two groups of people, one in

Thomas

Tennessee and one in Rockway, shot each other during the recovery says more about them than it does about the plan itself.

And I had wrongly assumed that Tamara was utterly haphazard in her planning. When she killed Jayne, she was working from a successful template, her stepfather's death in Saskatchewan. And I had to admit the backup dognapping plan was ingenious in a way. Tamara had introduced a dash of the bizarre into the story—the inflatable sheep—which was an effective bit of stage-magician misdirection.

Blaise and I listened to our phone messages, then I took him outside again to pee on car tires, just to kill time until the pet store opened. At nine o'clock we purchased a doggie bed, two bowls and a bag of ridiculously priced medicated kibble. The woman who managed the pet food store didn't seem at all surprised that I had a sudden need for those items.

"Blaise likes these," she said, holding up a mummified pig's ear. I don't know why the manager had one of those things lying on the counter beside her cash register. Maybe she nibbled on them between customers.

My paralegal task for that day was knocking on one hundred and twenty-six townhouse doors to arrange to have the fridges and stoves replaced. A pamphlet service could have delivered written notices for about two dollars, but I was getting tenant signatures acknowledging the upgrades. I may have mentioned that there was a loophole in The Landlord and Tenant Act that allowed rent controls to be circumvented after significant renovations. The new appliances would seem like a generous gesture until the tenants received their lease renewals. The delivery acknowledgements they signed would be used to defend any future legal challenge.

The old fridges and stoves were destined to be used in another, truly ancient, development, passed down like worn out hockey equipment from sibling to sibling.

Blaise was very helpful on that assignment because he dampened the natural suspicions of the tenants. I guess they figured that no one accompanied by a cute little dog could actually be a heat-seeking mamba.

Before Blaise and I drove home, we visited his old house to see if Karsci and Tamara really had pulled up stakes. As we approached, the windows told me that the house was empty. Houses get sad just like people do, and this split level was almost crying. Blaise climbed out of the truck and happily sniffed around the familiar yard, but he didn't seem inordinately sad. Maybe getting drugged and left in an attic for a day and a half took the glow off his relationship with his old masters.

When I opened the passenger door of the Chevy,

Thomas

Blaise bounded back into the cab, no visible regrets. I drove towards the lake and saw Henry Bourne and Snoopy sauntering along the fire lane. Henry was holding his shotgun casually underneath his left arm as if he had no intention of ever shooting it. I stopped and let Blaise out.

The two dogs took turns sniffing butts and seemed genuinely happy to see each other.

"I see your friend has moved," Henry said.

"Yeah. How did you know about it?"

"Karsci told me they were relocating, the other day. We met . . . geez, it was right about here and he said something about Montreal. He also said you'd be taking the dog." Grass rustled in the nearby ditch and Henry let the shotgun slide a little lower towards his hand. "A real estate guy has been walking around the property taking notes. I imagine the sign will be going up soon."

Blaise and I both shivered at the same time. There was no disputing it, Autumn was here and wasn't going to be shoved around by summer, anymore. Henry talked about the sky changing over the lake, like someone might talk about changing the curtains in a basement apartment and I nodded as if I understood what he meant.

As Blaise and I drove away, we heard a loud gunshot and a single pheasant flickered across my rear-view mirror.

Sib, Lacey, and I were talking about the case in Miele's over breakfast one Saturday, and Ilene gave us four coffee re-fills so she could hear more of the story. Lately, I had been compulsively tying up loose ends and I had to tell other people so they could see how clever I was. For example, I re-visited Trudy at Speedy Delivery and she eventually remembered Tamara dropping off a box for delivery, the day Blaise was supposedly dognapped. Trudy didn't make the connection immediately, because Tamara was a regular customer.

And I had more information from Mrs. Adamovich in the Farewell Creek-Tecumseh library. She said that Tamara's stepbrother, Alex, had no claim on the hundred-grand life insurance payout she received. Mrs. Adamovich didn't like the Zahradnik family very much and was glad that Tamara had made a clean break from the area. I don't know why I was so keen to prove that Tamara wasn't a thief when I had already demonstrated she was a murderer.

Benjamin Franklin would have understood the impulse. He said that being a "reasonable" person meant you could always find a reason to justify whatever you already believed. I had liked Tamara for three years and didn't want to completely overhaul that initial impression.

The only strong criticism I had of Tamara's behavior (now that I wasn't worried about her killing me) was that she had abandoned her little dog in her desire to relocate. Maybe the Polats were worried they could be traced through Blaise's Kennel Club registration, but it still seemed heartless and unnecessary to me.

Lacey didn't see it as inconsistent, however. "Tamara shot a high school acquaintance in the chest," she reminded me, "and she probably popped her father as well. She's capable of leaving a dog behind."

"Stepfather," I said. "She shot her stepfather." Words are important.

"Gopher—groundhog—whatever." Parents were a hot button topic for Lacey. She had mentioned her mom several times, but never her father.

None of my friends ever suggested telling the police about what I uncovered with my investigation. I found that a little odd because people are usually quite conservative and law-abiding, as long as the law affects other people. Everyone seemed to accept the fact that Tamara had cause to shoot Mitch Jayne and leave his body as coyote chow, there was no moral dilemma.

Of course, our conversation always circled back to the sheep because that's what made the story unique. Family members abused each other all the time, people blackmailed each other, and people shot each other. That was old news. But how many people used an inflatable sheep as an instrument of justice?

Ilene gave a final stamp of approval to Tamara's actions: "That's what I call thinking outside the box."

I drove Lacey to the Bo-Teek for a meeting with a potential business partner, someone who wanted Lacey to distribute *Tramp Magazine* through her mail order network.

"What's the matter?" She could tell that something was bothering me.

"Real detectives aren't supposed to rely on luck and happenstance."

"That's nonsense. Ted Bundy was pulled over in a routine traffic stop." We'd discussed his August arrest at an earlier breakfast session. "That piece of policework was more dependent on luck than anything you did." She reached over to pat my hand. "You have weirdly high standards for someone with a forged degree in business ethics..."

I shouldn't have told her about that.

"... from Texas Christian University."

Later that evening, I was in Lacey's apartment and there was no linguistic wiggle-room about what was happening. Blaise was lying in his doggie bed and would occasionally look up, raise an eyebrow then shudder.

The doorbell rang and I learned that Lacey and I shared a bizarre obsession. When we heard a phone ring, a car honk or a doorbell chime, we had to answer the call, there was simply no possibility of rolling over and wishing the person would go away.

I got my pants and shirt on in record time and pulled her door open.

Jack Sully, the man who had delivered the inflatable sheep to Karsci's house, was on the landing and he was holding a package. "Woah!" he said, recognizing me, "I come in peace." He held out the package which was too small to hold anything larger than an inflatable guinea pig.

"Hey," Lacey said, over my shoulder.

"Hey," Sully said. Obviously, they recognized each other, and I immediately wondered if Sully was a Dial-A-Feel customer. I turned and saw that Lacey had a robe on, not one of her own products, rather something she had stolen from the Radisson hotel in New York. It was voluminous and fluffy, without unnecessary holes or trim.

"Would you like a coffee?" Lacey had made a pot earlier, but circumstances had delayed the drinking.

"Sure." We all sat down at Lacey's kitchen table, got Ero-Teek mugs with copyright-infringing Felix-the-cat faces and started slurping away. Lacey carefully unwrapped her parcel like a kid who wasn't used to getting presents and wanted to prolong the pleasure. Sully and I waited patiently and eventually saw a book revealed: Peter Singer's *Animal Liberation*. Lacey turned to the title page and read an inscription: "to Lacey DeValera, a beautiful soul." It was signed by the author.

Then the book flopped open to a chapter called "Becoming a Vegetarian" because there was a hundred-dollar bill marking the place. Lacey turned a page and found another hundred-dollar bill. And another, and another. Ultimately, she had twenty miniature portraits of Robert Borden lined up on the kitchen table. The ex-prime minister looked slightly peeved, as if he had just been pulled from an over-priced rubber novelty.

"Thank you," Lacey said.

"You're welcome." Sully seemed genuinely happy to be the bearer of good news. He obviously remembered the note Karsci had shoved in his face a few weeks ago, because he smiled and said "that's dog ransom money."

I'd fully realized that Tamara was the architect of the phony dognapping scam when she signed out her copy of *Animal Liberation* the same day the ransom note was composed.

Tamara and/or Karsci had obviously sent this book as a "thank you" present for giving them time to slip away. They must have bumped into Dr. Singer on his North American book tour and got him to sign it. But why send it to Lacey instead of me?

"Maybe they thought you wouldn't accept the money," Lacey suggested, as if she had been reading my mind.

"Maybe." Secretly, I thought there was a threat wrapped in the money, like my mom used to hide tiny, super-hot sausages in a rolled pancake. The Polats were letting me know that they knew my girlfriend's address. They shouldn't have known I had a girlfriend, in the first place. I briefly wondered if I should contact Peter Singer's agent and see if he had attended any book signings near Montreal recently. But really, there was no reason to hunt the Polats down like ditch-pheasants. I should just enjoy my newfound freedom.

I had finally busted out of my pen. "I'm a ram sheep, baby," I said, "I'm a curly-horned devil"

Lacey recognized Junior Johnson's tune. "My hooves are made of steel, I'm as stubborn as I can be."

Sully joined in: "I want to get next to ewe, try to get next to me."

Dog nails snicked on kitchen linoleum, and Blaise looked up at us with a degree of interest but didn't take the next verse. Three Felix-the-cats winked as we raised mugs to our lips.

Next to Ewe

Oh, by the way, Sib's new girlfriend wasn't technically a nurse, she was a dental hygienist. He'll learn, soon enough, that precise definitions are important.

Acknowledgements

I'd like to thank Abby for seeing some potential in the book.
(It's not a conventional read)

Mark Thomas is a retired English and Philosophy teacher and ex-member of Canada's national rowing team. He has been shortlisted three times for Crime Writers of Canada Awards. Check out his work at https://flamingdogshit.com

Printed in the USA
CPSIA information can be obtained
at www.ICGtesting.com
LVHW031641070924
790362LV00016B/337

9 781958 901977